The President's Daughter

Terry Rajan

CCB Publishing
British Columbia, Canada

The President's Daughter

Copyright ©2008 by Terry Rajan
ISBN-13   978-0-9809191-2-7
First Edition

Library and Archives Canada Cataloguing in Publication

Rajan, Terry
The President's Daughter / written by Terry Rajan.
ISBN 978-0-9809191-2-7
I. Title.
PS8635.A455P74 2008   C813'.6   C2008-901373-5

United States Copyright Office Registration # TXu 1-024-954

Publisher: CCB Publishing
             British Columbia, Canada
             www.ccbpublishing.com

Chapter 1

The Democratic Primary

In downtown Seattle, Washington, The Democratic Head-quarters of Governor Johnson was awash with excitement. The dignified politician was preparing to celebrate his victory of winning the first twenty-two states Democratic Primary in the forth coming Presidential election. Richard Johnson was a tall slender man with deep expressive eyes that were warm and engaging. He was an attractive man with curly auburn hair framing a strong face with a confident smile. Anyone fortune to share a few private moments with the Governor felt their words were being taken seriously and were of importance to the esteemed politician. This ability to charm the general public with his company was a wonderful asset for any politician and with Richard Johnson that concern was sincere.

He was one of those rare politicians whose honesty, integrity and style of management served to command respect from the people he served. Richard Johnson was accepted as a good Christian man having demonstrated many years as a loving husband and father; he was a man deeply admired by millions of people. Governor Johnson would be making national news this evening. This was a rare opportunity for those other than the habitual C-SPAN viewers to listen to a fine politician. Richard Johnson was taking this opportunity to introduce himself to the nation.

Due to Richard's many political successes and innovative

policies within his home state he had long been advised to run for the Presidency. Richard's credentials were seemingly impeccable; his popularity among the people of the State of Washington hard to dispute. Although not yet termed-out as Governor it was thought by many that his policies were needed on a national level. Numerous polls conducted by his campaign staffers demonstrated that should Richard Johnson run for the Office of President, he could possibly win with the highest percentage of votes in history. Governor Johnson was clearly the Democratic front-runner for the Presidency in this year's Primaries having won twenty-two Democratic Primaries. Currently only Tom Gibson was the closest candidate to Governor Johnson in the number of votes cast. Political pundits, the press, and Democratic supporters were eagerly awaiting the announcement. Every media camera was focused on the podium. The hall was replete with banners displaying Governor Johnson's image.

Michael Wilson was also attending within his capacity as a political reporter for The Seattle Times-Sentinel. Due to his status he was seated front row centre beside Seattle Mayor Royal Hemmings. As the two men acknowledged one another there remained another half an hour before Richard's impending announcement. The Mayor leaned into Michael and whispered, "How much do you want to bet that our Governor Johnson will easily win the presidency?"

Wilson regarded him for several moments wearing a puzzled expression. "Mayor, why do you have so much confidence in Johnson?" he responded in a low voice.

Mayor Hemmings thought carefully prior to replying. He knew Wilson, as a reporter, had a well-deserved reputation as a political ball-breaker. In addition Mayor Wilson was painfully aware that Governor Johnson was one of this reporter's favorite targets.

"Governor Johnson has done more to bring the State of Washington into the public eye than anyone before him. His desire to work *for* the people has always felt genuine to me and

6

that, I can tell you, is a rare quality with career politicians."

As an experienced reporter Michael wasn't convinced by the Mayor's support of Richard. In an almost sneering tone, he asked, "Robert Newman is currently the Vice-President and has extensive national exposure as well as experience with D.C.'s political infighting. Governor Johnson is a novice to Washington D.C. politics and to the national media. What makes you believe that Johnson can compete with Newman's credentials? Of even greater importance how will Johnson's family values-first platform stand up to national scrutiny? You know a lot of people will be digging into his past."

Hemmings thought to himself, *'And especially you, you muck-raking son of a bitch!'* The Mayor, ever the professional, held his tongue. He then shifted the mood with his voice by reflecting a joking tact with Wilson. "Are you telling me that we all have some hidden agenda?"

The reporter's features twisted into a predatory gaze. "Run for the presidency yourself and we'll find out. You've been married twice, you have six children, you're rich." Wilson paused, "What are you worth, about 20 million? It's been said you're connected with Bill Gates, right?"

Hemmings body language changed indicating he was slightly uncomfortable. The Mayor glanced around him wishing he'd been assigned a different seat.

"I'm just a Mayor of another American town; nobody is ready for my politics yet. Where do you get your information anyway?"

Michael replied, "That's what I do for a living. Find the best and bring out the worst of people in power. You have heard of the First Amendment, correct?"

"What a way to earn money," Hemmings responded sarcastically.

Michael continued, "We all need food, shelter, sex, love and of course money to obtain the necessities in life. People with power have the same requirements, however, when they run for a public office it then becomes my business to check them out. Despite their intelligence, energy, and self confidence in my experience seldom are they free from skeletons rattling in their closets. It's a by-product of what they have achieved. They think that their wealth protects them from a painful history but in reality no one obtains political power without stepping on *someone*."

Hemmings harrumphed at the reporter's stinging comment.

'*A political reporter with a moral imperative. That's a new one!*' he shook his head sadly and turned his attention to the podium.

Their conversation ceased as the crowd hushed. Clapping began as Sue Jacob, Campaign Manager for Richard Johnson stepped to the podium. Sue had been with Richard since the earliest days of his run for Governor. She was 47 years old, a compactly built woman who consistently mirrored a trustworthy image of total competence. As a key component in the Governor's career Richard believed without her he'd never have achieved the same level of political success.

Sue Jacob addressed the crowd, "Ladies and gentlemen please welcome the next President of the United States, Richard Johnson!"

She stepped back from the podium, applauding with the crowd as she moved off to the side. With a warm smile Richard Johnson approached the podium with his family following close behind. Clapping and cheering began, swelling in volume as Richard stepped to the microphone. Governor Johnson listened to the warm support of his people permitting their greeting to continue for a moment before motioning for silence.

At precisely 7:00 p.m., the time designated for the celebration, silence reigned with a palpable sense of anticipation. Millions of people were watching the live broadcast on television as Richard walked confidently across the stage to the podium. He stepped up to the microphones and began to speak.

"Good evening. I wish to extend my gratitude to everyone for working so hard to make this event possible. Due to your efforts we have won the twenty-two states Democratic Primary for the office of the President of the United States of America."

The room erupted in applause and cheers. The celebration continued for several minutes longer while the Governor drank in their adoration. Richard then turned around to wink at his family seated directly behind him on the podium. His wife Donna, 23-year-old son Doug, and 22-year-old daughter Michelle warmly responded to his personal gesture. Doug was in graduate school studying political science at the University of Washington. Michelle was planning to be a nurse and was in attendance at the same University. The Governor's family was priceless to him and despite the toll fame had taken in robbing them of a private life his family was supportive of his political career. As the applause faded he returned his attention to the receptive audience.

"Thank you all, so much, for your confidence in me. I especially want to thank my lovely wife, Donna, and our wonderful children. Growing up in a public forum is difficult for any child. My own children have dealt with the public nature of my career with a grace and maturity far beyond their years. Without their love and support, I would not be standing before you today. There is a saying, 'Behind every successful man, there is a strong woman' and in my life that has certainly been true. She's right here with me tonight."

He walked over reaching for Donna's hand and brought it up to his lips for a warm kiss. Donna smiled up at him with tears forming in her eyes as the crowd again went wild with excitement. Richard returned to the microphones. He began by clearing his throat having been visibly overwhelmed with emotion from the warm response from his many supporters.

"My son Doug and daughter Michelle bring pure joy to their mother and myself. They have understood and accepted my hectic schedule which has deprived our family of much personal time. I can never thank them enough for their constant support as they have been sharing their dad with the State of Washington, and from now on with the entire United States of America."

He turned towards his children and smiled, then turned back to address the crowd further.

"My family believes in me. They believe, just as I do, that we can make a difference in this world." Richard stated these words emphatically, firmly gesturing with the classic military drill sergeant gesture: upper two fingers pointed outward, lower fingers folded under. Richard seldom employed this gesture of strength however at this pivotal moment he was determined to drive home one of his essential core values: the family.

As another round of applause began, he joined in, clapping his hands in the direction of his wife and children. He then turned back to the cluster of microphones. We know the other Democratic candidates have all dropped out of the primary race leaving Tom Gibson as the only remaining candidate. He is hard working and will not take this race lightly or will quit easily. He has the personal financial backing of his own money including rich powerful friends and corporations supporting him. Tom Gibson's millions should not serve to intimidate us; we must, however maintain the momentum for people to understand our mission. I have a new vision for this country. I am a going to make the United States of America the greatest and most respected nation in the world.

"My platform and priorities are, first and foremost, to protect the safety of every American. I will improve our economy, and raise the standard of living for every person in this country. I pledge to each and every one of you that as President I will work hard to improve the current educational programs in this country. It cannot be taken for granted that education is an essential element in improving our country's standard of living. It is my mission to enable young people with an opportunity for growth by becoming engineers, scientists, teachers, and doctors. In additional I will work hard to improve the Medicare system to enable everyone, including the elderly and poor to benefit from an adequate health care plan."

Governor Johnson continued, his passion growing in intensity with each passing second. "My style of government is to *not* take from business and give to the people; *nor* is it to take from the people and give to business. My policy is to work *together* to develop a 'win-win' situation for everyone wherever possible. Insurance companies' initial concerns should rest with educating the public by promoting safety and health standards; not with company profit margins. The people then win by experiencing fewer accidents, reduced insurance premiums and improved personal health. The insurance companies will win by passing these savings along to the people; this will result in prosperity for families. We do *not* want to build additional prisons to house criminals; we want to build better *schools* to educate our young people. In this manner with a better education students will refrain from temptation and will not be enticed by a career which includes criminal activity. We want to keep everyone working and give back hope and pride to the people of America. I want *everyone* to join me to become actively involved in improving our country. We will fight for democracy and human rights for all the people of the world. Minority oppression by governments and dictators must be stopped! We have hard work ahead for us and it will most likely be a long and hard campaign. But I am certain we will emerge victorious and, with your support, we will win this campaign by a landslide! Thank you everyone for your faith in me!"

With the sound from the crowd's thunderous applause, Richard turned retracing his steps back to join his waiting family. Donna rose to her feet and warmly took her husband's hand. The couple with their two children standing on either side of them, turned to the crowd waving; together the family then moved away from the podium.

Waiting for them backstage were many of their friends and fellow politicians gathered together to offer their support and congratulations. As his supporters crowded around shaking Richard's hand and patting him on the back, he thought, *"How can I lose with all of these wonderful people supporting me?"* He knew the importance of this unique moment in his life, this was a night to remember. Donna moved next to her husband and taking his hand into her own gave him an intimate squeeze. He sensed she also understood the importance of this occasion and knew precisely how he was feeling at the same moment. They walked across the center of the room to a table which held a gigantic cake displaying the Governor's picture; beneath his image it read, "Richard Johnson for President."

It was precisely at that moment that the impact of the occasion hit Richard. He had just officially announced to the world that he, Richard Johnson, was the popular Democratic candidate for President of the United States. Everything suddenly appeared surreal. He glanced across the room identifying members of his family and friends, Lieutenant Governor Ronald Jennings, Mayor Hemmings, and the competent people that composed his campaign staff.

He tried speaking to them but briefly paused for a moment. Governor Johnson was clearly overwhelmed with emotion from the outpouring of faith in his abilities to lead the nation. As Richard addressed his supporters he was immediately provided with respectful silence.

"It is indeed an honor to be standing in this room with you tonight. Thank you for your role in assisting me to reach this pivotal moment in my political career. This occasion means the world to me, everyone please accept my gratitude for your continued support. However we are far from winning the Democratic nomination as a difficult fight lies ahead. I believe we are up to the task. With your support I *will be* the next President of the United States of America! In leading this great nation we will accomplish our goals and achieve everything we have lobbied for!"

Richard and Donna made the rounds of his supporters attempting to speak to everyone personally that night. Doug soon approached his parents to inform them of his plans; he and a group of friends were leaving for a popular nightclub to celebrate.

Richard teased him asking "And you're not inviting me?"

"Yeah right Dad!" He laughed. He gave his parents each a quick hug before heading back to his friends.

As Doug walked across the room, he paused for a moment to briefly study Caroline Hoffman. She was standing with a group of his friends enjoying herself. Although only 25, Caroline held the coveted campaign position as his father's personal assistant. In working with the Governor she had also become close to their family. Doug had known her for almost six months however he'd hidden all traces that he was crazy about her. Caroline didn't appear to regard him as any more than a friend, he was however working on plans to change her perception of him. *'She is gorgeous'*, he thought, especially with her long hair curled down around her shoulders. Although she usually wore her auburn hair up tonight she looked hot and rather seductive. Caroline had warm expressive eyes and a beautiful smile; she was hands down the most beautiful woman he knew. For the occasion she had worn a cream-colored silk blouse with a brown and cream skirt. Intrigued by the texture he had casually touched it earlier when they'd briefly spoken. It was a silky fabric with a flirty hem, short enough to look sexy but not inappropriate for the occasion. She always dressed classy like that and he realized that there wasn't a thing about this woman that he didn't find appealing. Doug made his way over to the group and placed his arm around Caroline's shoulders.

"So are you are ready to go?" Doug asked.

Caroline answered, "In a minute, just let me say goodbye first!"

She made her way across the room to exchange a warm hug with her esteemed boss. Caroline's spontaneous gesture placed an immediate smile on the Governor's face. His wife and daughter were silently observing and additionally sharing the same unspoken thought. *'She may work with him, but this doesn't seem right?'*

Caroline turned with a quick smile and asked, "Mr. President, may I have your permission to go to a nightclub with Doug and his friends?"

"You may, but keep an eye out for anyone driving under the influence!" he replied.

"Yes sir, I will!" she shyly glanced up at him before adding, "You made a wonderful speech tonight sir." Caroline turned and walked back towards Doug.

As they were leaving the hall, Doug called out to his sister, "Coming?" Michelle glanced over quickly assessing the situation between her brother and his friends. He may be a year older than her but sometimes he seemed so painfully immature.

"No, I think I'll take a pass," she replied.

Caroline spoke up, "Come on Michelle, it's going to be fun!"

Michelle shook her head in reply, "No forget it, I know how you guys can get! Have fun though!"

As a sister she was well aware of Doug's crush, she also knew his feelings were not reciprocated by Caroline. Michelle didn't like admitting she was often jealous of the young woman. Lately Caroline seemed to be including herself in everything, practically becoming a member of their family. Michelle had grown to believe that even her parents adored the young assistant, almost as much as Doug. She was a nice person but lately as a family they were seldom alone, especially with Caroline always tagging along. Her brother was forever going on about "Caroline this" and "Caroline that," while her father gave glowing reports of her daily accomplishments at the campaign office. She was simply tired of listening about the "wonderful Caroline" it just seemed endless. *"Well,"* she mused, *"tonight I'll have my parents all to myself."* She approached her mother asking, "Are you ready to head home yet?"

Donna replied, "I thought you would be going with Doug and Caroline?"

Her mother was aware of the times Michelle appeared somewhat envious of Caroline however she wanted to believe they were still close. Michelle had her own beauty, quite different from

Caroline, she was also a gifted and sensitive young woman. She wore her sandy brown hair in a short fashionable style that framed her large green eyes. Michelle had a cute little figure and had always been very popular, she had little trouble finding male companionship when she wanted it. Donna had carefully watched them together but couldn't understand her daughter's apparent jealousy of Caroline.

"How come you didn't go to the club with the others, honey?" Donna asked her daughter.

"Oh Mom, you know how they can get. I'm not really into the nightclub scene. I thought it might be nice to just spend the evening at home; Dad is about to go for his interview with Bill O'Reilly. I thought I would just go home and watch him on TV."

Michelle looked through the crowds seeking her father's familiar profile. She finally located him engrossed in a deep discussion with several of his staff members on the other side of the room. She made her way over to him with her mother following close behind. Standing next to her dad she waited for a break in the conversation when she knew he'd take a few moments just for her.

She hugged her father and then proudly gave him encouragement, "Dad, good luck, stick to the subject; keep your answers short and on point. Don't let him bait you."

"Thank you dear, I'll try my best. You know how O'Reilly can be." He could see the love and pride reflected on his daughter's lovely face. She adored her father and as always she was right. The evening was by no means over yet. Richard embraced the two of them and then watched as his daughter turned and walked away with her mother.

'She's always watching out for me,' he thought.

He motioned to Sue Jacob that it was time to leave for the interview. They had discussed their game plan days ago; Sue would be accompanying him to ensure that he stayed on point and didn't allow O'Reilly to antagonize him. Governor Johnson was totally focused on his first national appearance. This major television interview was just the beginning and Governor Johnson intended to delivery his message to the nation with total perfection. Appearances meant everything in the world of politics; there were never any second chances.

Chapter 2

The Opposition

Across town, Democratic Congressman Tom Gibson watched the TV announcement of the impending Johnson interview with interest. As a long-time political rival of Richard Johnson they shared a grudging respect for each other, a mutual truth that neither would publicly acknowledge. Richard's politics tended to be too liberal for Gibson, who fancied himself a true conservative Democrat. They had jousted many times over different issues, in particular the fiscal concerns of Washington State. This however was different as Richard had beaten him to the punch with his straight twenty-three state-winning announcement. An hour later Gibson settled back into his chair planning his own campaign strategies as the O'Reilly TV interview began.

"This should be interesting", Gibson mused with contentment. *"O'Reilly's gonna tear him apart."*

In the Johnson home, Donna and Michelle were equally engaged watching the O'Reilly interview. This was Richard's first national interview following his candidacy announcement; it was imperative he got off on the right foot and never allow O'Reilly to steer him off course. Michelle was aware she was nervous for her father; Bill O'Reilly was notorious during interviews for antagonizing those he considered liberal into revealing issues which often were later misinterpreted. Michelle took a cleansing breath and silently prayed for her father. Her mother reached over and gently squeezed her hand in an attempt to reassure them both.

Richard sat beneath the bright warm lights of the studio, attempting to compose himself. As Governor his history included a confident track record of many successful interviews; however never of this importance.

Richard smiled to himself *"And Bill O'Reilly to boot!"* his thoughts turned to the interview *"Tonight of all nights I refuse to let my emotions get the better of me."*

One of O'Reilly's staffers signaled that it was time to begin, "counting down: "3, 2, and… you're on."

O'Reilly addressed the camera to introduce his distinguished company. "My guest tonight is Washington State Governor Richard Johnson. Governor Johnson just won the first twenty-two states Democratic Primary for the Democratic nomination for President." He turned towards Richard, "Congratulations on your victory Governor."

Richard warmly smiled. He also concentrated on holding his gaze to not blink while adjusting to the harshness of the studio lights "Thank you and thank you for providing this opportunity."

O'Reilly began his questions. "What convinced you to run for the Presidency, Governor?"

Richard carefully folded his hands in his lap, looked directly into the camera, and replied:

"The future of every American including my own family. I am truly concerned with the decline of the American nuclear family over the past few decades. Economic pressures have forced many families into situations which necessitates that both parents must work. This in turn naturally decreases the quality of time spent nurturing their children. As a result, juvenile criminal and drug issues are on the rise, divorce rates are higher than they ever have been…"

O'Reilly cut Richard off in mid-sentence. "So you want to become President just to make sure *your* children will have a good future."

Richard did not rise to the bait. He calmly replied, "In short, yes. However my thoughts are long term in this regard and do not simply concern my own family."

O'Reilly quickly changed direction. He realized the Governor wasn't going to respond as he had anticipated.

"Let's discuss your two most likely opponents? Tom Gibson has powerful friends including the advantage of a considerable sum of personal wealth. You must also agree that Vice-President Newman has the benefit of experience...experience which you simply don't have?" O'Reilly paused briefly for effect, "Governor Johnson, why then should people vote for you?"

Richard carefully considered his response. He silently calmed himself prior to replying.

"Vision. A *long-term* vision for America. I believe that Tom Gibson and Vice-President Newman lack a clear, definable vision of where America should be in 10, 20 or 50 years. I try to look at the big picture to find a long term, lasting solution to issues. Any nation that wants to be great needs a system that becomes institutionalized; one that is not dependent on any one party or person to keep it running effectively. That is my long-term vision for America."

O'Reilly continued, "You've stated in many of your speeches that one of your priorities is to reduce unemployment. Exactly how do you attend on achieving that goal?"

"And so it begins," Richard thought. *"Stay calm, stick to what you know and don't worry about O'Reilly. He's just a mouthpiece."*

"The American middle-class is the backbone of this country. They form much of America's tax base. It is therefore crucial to keep them employed working within situations that allow them to advance, *not* just a job where they are forced to struggle living paycheck to paycheck. We *need* to eliminate the term working-poor from our vocabulary. Large portions of our people have families without health or retirement benefits. They may have jobs, however they are not provided with any essential benefits. I will initiate programs that will provide tax benefits to companies that demonstrate they are willing to grow here in the U.S. Companies that will not export jobs outside of our country for cheap labor; companies that will provide benefits to their employees in the U.S., specifically health and retirement benefits. This will increase productivity, reduce company taxes, reduce government social security payload and reduce unemployment. When this is taken into consideration the companies win, the people win and the government wins."

O'Reilly rolled his eyes at the camera, indicating his disdain for Richard's opinion. Richard caught the look as he was speaking, but let it pass.

O'Reilly decided to change course again, "Let's explore another sensitive issue. Where do you stand on abortion?"

This was one of those 'make or break' questions. Richard assessed the need of being observed in a manner that provided weight to his response without totally avoiding the issue.

"Sensitive issues like abortion never *have* a simple answer. There are however several variables that must be carefully considered. First: the rights of the woman. She may not want the child because her pregnancy was the result of rape or incest. Second: Do we really know when life begins? Third: Who should be responsible for taking care of an unwanted child? I'm not aware of any anti-abortionists stepping up to adopt these children in lieu of abortion. It is my belief though that each and every case deserves to be carefully considered. We shouldn't have a universal answer. Richard paused for several moments then continued using a quiet and sincere tone of voice, "I hardly believe there is sufficient time for a neither lengthy explanation nor may your viewers wish to listen to a solution for every case in detail."

O'Reilly stared at Richard like a bug he wanted to squash. "So you're saying that you support abortion?"

Richard firmly repeated, "I am a good Christian and against abortion, but I support the idea that there is no universal way to resolve this issue without offending someone. I am a person who believes in the individual rights of the person. I'd respectfully prefer to leave it at that."

O'Reilly once more quickly switched the topic. His attempts to trip Richard up were quite obvious but unsuccessful. This was one of the qualities that made Richard such a successful and believable politician; he stuck to his guns when he believed in something and was not easily intimidated.

"How will you handle international policy? I would believe as the Governor of Washington, you've been involved for the most part with only domestic affairs. Tell our viewers how you plan to manage some of our more pressing international issues; terrorism, the falling value of the dollar, etc."

Richard turned away from O'Reilly and addressed his response directly to the camera.

"Your point may be valid that due to the nature of my position as Governor much of my political experience has been of domestic origin. However, I have also been involved in many foreign policy decisions some of which I supported while others I opposed. As Governor of Washington, we enacted a sister-city program in Japan, Brazil, and Chile, to simply name a few. This attracted an interest from foreign companies bringing investments into our state, which then resulted in additional employment. My work as Governor has taken me all over the world." Richard paused anticipating an interruption. When O'Reilly remained silent he then continued.

"My policy regarding international politics is not necessarily 'your enemy is my enemy' or my enemy should be yours just because we may be allies. I firmly believe in dealing with each country in as individual a manner as possible. I question myself as to what it may do to our country. Am I ready to sacrifice young sons and fathers simply to achieve superiority? Definitely and absolutely not. Are you aware of how many children, wives, mothers and fathers have lost loved ones in our battle to maintain U.S. superiority? Have you taken into consideration the number of children who have been maimed and lost limbs or are coping with traumatic emotional issues? In addition divorce and suicide rates are considered far too high in respect to our soldiers? The issue must be raised are we looking after them well enough? Are we providing them with adequate medical care?"

O'Reilly attempted to interject however Governor Johnson quickly cut him of. He stated "Don't misunderstand me, though. I *will* use necessary force as Commander-in-Chief to defend our way of life if it is being *legitimately* threatened. Let's understand something; all the freedom-fighting groups are not terrorists. One man's terrorist is another man's freedom fighter. The line between terrorist groups and freedom fighting groups is a matter of perception. Bill, don't cut me off, and please listen to this carefully: A good example is Sri Lanka's Liberation Tigers of Tamil Eelam, the LTTE. You must understand the reason for their fight. My physician is a Sri Lankan Tamil. "During an office consultation I asked him, "Do support the Tamil rebel group LTTE?"

Initially he appeared amused and then replied, "You must first have an understanding of our history before forming any conclusions. In 1948 when Sri Lanka gained its independence from the British the majority imperiled minority Tamil's linguistic rights. The rights to education and employment; it additionally deprived them of their rights to ownership of their traditional lands. Are you aware that it further endangered their religious and cultural life? As a direct consequence this sequence of events posed a serious threat to their very rights to a decent humane existence. As an integral part of the genocidal program, the state organized periodical communal holocausts. This situation plagued the island, resulting in mass extermination of Tamils and massive destruction of their property. They raped, looted and killed many innocent minority Tamils. There was no LTTE at that time. Understand that LTTE was born because of this situation. My concern is why at that time didn't the U.S., or any other country for that matter, including the United Kingdom take the appropriate action?"

Richard continued, "So I researched and soon confirmed that

22

everything my physician had said was indeed true."

"To separate a freedom fighter from a terrorist may not be easy however it can be done once the time is taken to understand their cause, history and culture. There are countries with arm dealers who have taken advantage of such situations by selling arms to the wrong governments and all in the name of wiping out terrorism."

"Indigenous peoples worldwide should have the same freedom and rights as the so-called dominant cultures. When you take these rights away there *will* be someone who will take a leadership position and fight. The issue of terrorism has many complex variables that require our peoples as a nation to make a conscientious effort in understanding other cultures before we label them as terrorists."

Bill O'Reilly quickly changed the subject and shot back, "Gay rights, where do you stand?" O'Reilly then flashed a quick grin at Richard. The Governor exuding a sense of self confidence acknowledged the grin then replied, "You know how to put someone in a corner don't you?"

"That *is* my job, Governor."

Richard chuckled while slightly shifting his position in the chair.

"Okay. Gay people deserve respect. The question is this: Do we provide them with additional rights simply due to their sexual orientation. I don't believe so, however, they do deserve to be treated fairly. Not having earned the degree of a biologist or doctor I am not qualified to speculate on what determines a person's sexual orientation. We should however never ignore nor discriminate against any minority. As a married man, with a family, I am not gay, nor am I a supporter or promoter of homosexuality. I do however believe in the principle of respecting alternative lifestyles. That is after all, the premise that America was built upon; freedom from discrimination for everyone including all minorities. If one of my children happened to be gay what would I do as their father? Abandon them? No, not a chance."

One of O'Reilly's set people gave the signal that time was up. O'Reilly turned to Richard, "Governor Johnson, thank you for taking the time to discuss these issues. I'm sure you will make this an interesting race. Good luck."

Richard, feeling satisfied that he had passed the first of what would be many tests in the media, replied "Thank you for having me. It was a pleasure."

Donna and Michelle warmly hugged each other in their family living room. "Dad did an awesome job!" Michelle exclaimed. "O'Reilly wasn't able to ruffle him at all."

Releasing her daughter Donna replied, "I'm so proud of your father. Since the first day I met him he's always been strong; unflappable in the face of the enemy. Let's hope he can keep it up, it's going to be a long hard road."

Tom Gibson had watched the interview with interest. Convinced that this would be the beginning of Richard's undoing, he was dismayed to see that the Governor had conducted himself as always: polite and dignified. Tom picked up the phone and placed a call to his own Campaign Manager, Josh Elliott.

"Josh, you need to get me on O'Reilly's show! Did you see Johnson's interview? He aced it! I think that would be the best place for me to announce my own policies and priorities. What do you think?"

Josh, never one to challenge his boss, replied, "I'll get right on it. When do you want to have the interview?"

Tom spoke with his Campaign Manager for several more minutes, then hung up the phone and sat down. He now realized that he might be in for a long battle for Democratic supremacy against a man like Richard Johnson.

"Now exactly when is it my turn?" He muttered bitterly.

Vice-President Newman's staff had not been idle, either. Everyone had watched Richard's interview with Bill O'Reilly developing a newfound respect for this Democratic upstart. They acknowledged that Newman would win the Republican nomination being more of a hard-liner. However they also knew that Richard's policies, as he had stated them in the interview, would resonate with the people of America.. Newman had not risen to the Office of Vice-President through natural political skill; rather he had used the barter system to get himself on the ticket seven years earlier. Even President Woodruff, considered a lame-duck President, had never treated Newman with the respect that Newman believed he deserved.

As they finished watching the interview, Newman came out of his office and entered the room. He was a short, balding, pompous little man who with narcissistic pleasure demanded constant attention. Truth be known he was more of an astute bargainer than politician for the people. He was a man better suited for the backrooms of D.C. than the ruse of any upfront exposure in leading the people.

"So, what do we do about this little piss-ant?" Newman boomed out to his staff.

One of Newman's 20 year veteran staff members tentatively suggested, "Sir, he didn't really give concrete answers to O'Reilly's questions on the abortion or gay rights issues. It sounded like he was playing both sides against the middle."

Newman peered at the man over his glasses, which characteristically were perpetually balanced on the end of his nose. An unflattering trait that his PR people had been trying to change for years.

"That's a good starting point. Contact the media people we use and give them our response to Johnson's interview. You know what to say."

"Yes sir, I'll get right on it." The staffer rushed out of the room to make the calls.

Newman regarded the remainder of his staff, attempting to surmise appropriately assigned duties. "If any of the rest of you have any contacts that can find anything on this guy, get to it!" They all fled to their tasks, leaving Newman alone in the room to mull over his options. He knew he could get some dirt on Johnson, it was one of the things he did best. His staff was well trained and unwavering in their loyalty to him. Newman returned to his office with his own agenda in mind. He was intent on conducting his own phone calls; he had contacts even his staffers knew nothing about.

Chapter 3

And So It Begins

Doug and Caroline and his friends Jeremy, Kevin and Beth got into Doug's car. Caroline sat up front next to Doug, and the rest piled into the back seat. Caroline went through Doug's CD collection, and asked what everyone wanted to hear. Everyone yelled out something different, so Caroline said "Never mind you goofballs, I'll decide!" She put in a Garth Brooks CD, and everyone started to sing along to *I've Got Friends in Low Places.* Doug glanced over at Caroline, and smiled. The irony of singing that particular song in light of the night's events was not lost on her, either. She slapped him playfully on the arm and said, "Watch the road silly."

He wanted her to like him as more than a friend, so why wouldn't she? He had asked her out many times, but the only times she would go out with him was when there was a group of them going together. He thought he was a fairly good looking guy, worked out five days a week; he considered himself to have a nice body. Nice abs, tight muscles. He had asked Michelle once that if he weren't her brother would she think he was an okay looking guy, and she had said he was. She said her friends all thought he was cute. So then why didn't Caroline? He looked over at her again, and she said "Come on, sing with us Doug!" Unable to resist her he joined in with them until they got to the club.

They all climbed out of the car and headed inside.

Doug stated, "Kevin and I will go order the drinks. I know

Jeremy wants a rum and coke, and Beth a Margarita. What would you like Caroline?"

"Just orange juice for me, Doug. I'll drive home tonight, okay?" Caroline replied. "Jeremy, will you grab a table while Beth and I freshen up?"

She and Beth headed over to the restrooms.

"So Beth, don't you think Jeremy looks cute tonight?" Beth just looked at Caroline and shook her head.

"Caroline, Doug is *so* in love with you! You just can't be flirting with Jeremy tonight! You *will* break Doug's heart because Jeremy is his best friend!" Beth could not figure out why Caroline did not go for Doug. He really *was* gorgeous. She wished he liked *her* instead of Caroline. She would go out with him in an instant. Maybe it was because Doug's dad was about to become President. It was one thing to be dating the Governor's son, but it would be really hard to date the President's son with all those Secret Service guys around all the time. "How come you don't go out with Doug, anyway? Is it because Mr. Johnson is running for President?"

"No, I'm on his campaign staff, so I'm dealing with all of that. Doug and I are just friends. I have no interest in him as a boyfriend. Why don't you go for it, Beth? Maybe you and Doug should go out! Then we could double date, you and Doug and me and Jeremy! That would be fun, huh?"

"Yeah right, Caroline." Beth rolled her eyes. "Like Doug has ever looked at anyone but you since you got to Seattle! He'll keep working on you until you break down and finally go out with him, and you know it, you brat!" Beth gave Caroline a playful shove, and said, "We better get back out there, before they send someone in here looking for us!"

They walked out into the club, looked around for the guys and found them at a table right next to the dance floor. As Caroline approached the table, Doug grabbed Caroline's hand and said, "Come on, dance with me!" She didn't want to embarrass him by turning him down in front of everyone, so she went with him. At least the music had a fast beat.

They danced two songs, and then Doug said, "Damn, I'm hot! Let's get another drink." He looked over at their table. "Oh, you haven't even touched yours yet! Well, you sit down. I'm going to get another one for myself. Anyone need another drink?" he asked as he headed off to the bar.

As Doug walked away, Caroline remarked, "Looks like Doug is having a good time. I'm glad I'm driving home tonight!"

Caroline glanced down at the table and saw that Doug had already had two drinks while she was in the restroom. She wondered why he was doing this. It was not like him.

"Jeremy, is Doug okay?"

Jeremy looked at her and said, "Yeah. He's probably just excited about his dad, and you said you would drive home, so he's probably thinking it's okay to drink a little more than usual, I guess." He looked at her with about as much subtlety as an oncoming freight train and exclaimed, "Come and dance with me!"

Caroline got up and went out on the dance floor with Jeremy. She was glad he asked her. She really liked him. A slow dance had just begun, so she went into Jeremy's arms. She looked up and saw Doug staring at them, and she felt bad. He looked really hurt, but maybe this was for the best. She had tried to make it clear they were just friends. She held Jeremy a little tighter, and laid her head on his shoulder. She saw Doug down his drink and with a mournful glance at the two of them, head to the bar for another. When the song ended, they headed back to the table.

Doug joined them a short time later and sat across from Caroline. When another slow song started playing, Doug took her hand and asked her to dance. She felt bad, so she agreed. They headed out on the dance floor. She tried to keep a distance between them as they danced, but Doug kept trying to pull her closer. He then put his hand on the back of her neck and started to kiss her.

Caroline yelled loudly, "What are you doing? I'm your sister! How could you?"

She pushed him away as hard as she could, eyes burning with

the coming tears, running blindly across the room, bumping into several people on her way out of the club. Doug just stood there for a moment; a shocked look on his face as Jeremy came running over to him.

"What did you do stupid? Go after her!"

Doug started for the door, and realized he had had too much to drink when he had trouble running in a straight line. His own vision blurred with tears of shame. The others ran along with him, and as they got out the door, they heard brakes screeching followed by a loud thud. Everyone started screaming, and Doug just felt sick. He ran over and tried to make his way through the crowd that had gathered around. Jeremy was right behind him, trying to push people out of their way. They got up to the scene of the accident and saw Caroline's body lying in the street, blood spilling from a gash on her head.

The driver of the van that had hit Caroline was kneeled down beside her as they all approached. "She came out of nowhere! I never had time to stop!" He turned to the gathering group and yelled, "Someone call 911!"

Beth got out her phone and called 911, only to find out that someone had already called and the ambulance was on the way.

Doug just stood there, screaming "What have I done, what have I done?" The anguish in his voice was felt by everyone around him.

Beth put her phone away and put her arms around Doug. Time froze, everyone and everything falling away for a moment. Jeremy took Doug's arm and led him over to Caroline. They heard sirens and the crowd started to move away. An ambulance pulled up and a pair of paramedics raced over to Caroline's body.

"Please let her be alive," Doug prayed, falling to his knees.

As one of the paramedics wheeled a gurney over, Doug called out, "Is she alive? Is she okay? It's all my fault, please say she is okay!"

Jeremy left Doug with Beth and went over and asked one of the paramedics to at least let them know if Caroline was alive. The paramedic confirmed that she was alive, but then asked Jeremy to step back. After working on Caroline for a few minutes they carefully put her on a stretcher, then loaded Caroline into the ambulance and told Jeremy they were taking her to Harborview Medical Center.

Jeremy walked over to Doug and the others and said, "Come on, we'll follow them to the hospital. Beth you can drive. Doug, give her your keys." He turned to Kevin, "Will you go inside and get our stuff?" Doug looked up at Jeremy with the glazed look of someone trying to make sense of something terrible, but getting nowhere.

Kevin ran back inside, got their things, and was back to the car in no time. They climbed back into the car, where they had been so happy and carefree just a couple hours ago, and headed for the hospital. This car ride was much different than the last. They rode in silence. No one said a word. Beth was crying as she drove, and Kevin was watching the road ahead to try to make sure she was driving okay. None of it seemed real. They all had the sense that powerful forces were in motion that they had no control over; forces that threatened to overwhelm the reasons behind tonight's celebration. They pulled up to the hospital, and hurried inside.

Inside the emergency room, several doctors and nurses were standing around Caroline treating her. She slowly regained consciousness.

She opened her eyes briefly, and asked one of the doctors, "Where is my dad?"

The doctor asked, "Who is your dad?"

Caroline replied, "Richard Johnson."

The doctor said, "The Governor of Washington?"

She replied, "Yes, where is he?"

The doctor said, "We will call him, don't worry. He is on his way."

He then told a nurse to go out and tell the police that she was the Governor's daughter, and he should be informed immediately. The nurse left the room to talk with the policeman who was there;

then she went to phone her boyfriend, Michael Wilson. Michael was a reporter for the Seattle Times-Sentinel, and she was certain this would be big news. He would have the first chance at the story.

The policeman called the Chief of Police at home and informed him of the accident. The Chief called Richard at his Seattle home to inform him of the bad news.

"Richard, I hate to have to be the one to tell you this, but Michelle has been in a car accident tonight. She is at Harborview Medical Center now. You better get over there right away."

Richard would have thought this was some kind of horrible joke, except he had known the chief for years and knew Tom's voice.

"Tom, there's some kind of mistake because Michelle is here with me. I'm looking at her right now. Who told you she was in a car accident?"

He then explained to Richard that one of his officers had called from the hospital saying that the doctors had said the girl in the accident claimed she was his daughter. Just then his cell phone rang, and he said, "Hold on a minute, Tom." He answered the other call, and it was Doug. He said he was calling from Harborview, and there had been an accident. Richard sat down, *'Oh no,'* he thought, *'it was his son, not his daughter.'*

Richard grappled with what he was hearing. "Doug, slow down. What happened?"

Doug was talking about it being all his fault, and how this could have happened, and Richard said again, trying to be reassuring, "Calm down Doug. Are you hurt?"

Doug then started speaking more slowly and explained that Caroline had been hit by a car and was in the emergency room. She had run out into the road and it was his fault.

Richard said, "Stay there Doug, I'm on my way."

Richard then got back on the phone and told the Police Chief, "Tom, it was not Michelle. It was one of my assistants, Caroline Hoffman. She was with my son tonight, so they must have just thought it was Michelle. I am heading for the hospital now."

The Chief said he would meet him there. Donna and Michelle both wanted to know what was going on, and Richard said, "Grab your coats. I'll fill you in on the way."

When Richard, Donna, and Michelle arrived, Doug was in the waiting room. He ran over and hugged his mom. She could smell the alcohol on his breath.

"Mom, this was all my fault! How could I have done this? What if she doesn't make it? What am I going to do?"

Donna hugged her son, trying to soothe him. "Doug, take a deep breath, and try to tell us the whole story."

While she was trying to calm Doug down, Richard and Michelle were trying to get information on Caroline's condition. They were told that she had a serious head injury, and she was currently in surgery. They would have to wait and see how she was. They walked over and joined Doug and Donna. They told Donna the news on Caroline, and then Doug began to fill them in. He was making an obvious attempt to try and sober up as he spoke.

"We left your party, and went to the club like I told you we would, Caroline, Beth, Kevin, Jeremy, and me. The girls went off to talk for a little bit, and the guys and I had a few drinks. Caroline and I danced for a while, and then when I went to get another drink, she started dancing with Jeremy. I guess I was jealous, so for the next slow song, I asked Caroline to dance again and got a little closer than she wanted me to. I tried to kiss her and she got mad and pushed me away and ran out of the club. I went after her and next thing I knew, she was hit by a car and in an ambulance on her way to the hospital! I know I should not have pushed myself on her, but I like her so much, Mom, and I want her to like me back!" Her son's grief tore at Donna.

Doug continued, "Not as just a friend, more than that! This is my fault, and now I may not even have her as a friend! What have I done? And if she makes it through the surgery, how do I make this up to her?"

Donna reached over and took hold of her son's shoulders.

"Caroline is very fond of you Doug. She will recover from this, and she will forgive you and remain your friend. You need to accept the fact that you are 'just friends' though, honey. You can't make someone love you, it either happens or it doesn't."

Tom walked into the room just then. He took Richard aside and said, "I need to talk to you a minute. I just spoke with some of the doctors and nurses that were in the emergency room with Caroline Hoffman, and she told them that you were her father, Richard."

Richard looked at him incredulously.

"She has a pretty bad head injury, maybe that was why she said it. You need to contact her family though, and let them know what has happened."

Richard had not thought of that. Pulling out his cell phone, he called his Campaign Manager, Sue Jacob, and told her about the accident. He asked her to go to headquarters and get Caroline's family information from the personnel files. He asked her to bring the info to the hospital, and he would call them himself. She agreed to do it right away.

A hospital administrator approached Richard and told him they would need some information on Caroline. He told her he would complete what he knew, and that his Campaign Manager would be there shortly with more information. She asked if he knew if Caroline had medical insurance, and he informed her that if there were none, he would personally pay her medical costs, pleading that they should just make sure she received the proper care. He walked back over to his family, and they sat and waited for news. As they waited, they talked of Caroline and how close they had all become. She had become like a member of the family in the short time they had known her.

Michelle started crying and said, "I feel bad now. I've been selfish because we don't get enough time together as a family, and Caroline always seems to be showing up at all our family get-togethers, making me resent her. How could I have been so selfish?"

Donna thought for a moment, then stated, "Don't feel bad Michelle. You have always been very nice to Caroline, I'm sure she did not realize how you felt." Donna tried to carefully consider her next words. "Maybe you two will become closer friends after she has recovered."

Richard was deep in thought wondering why Caroline would say she was his daughter. *'Her family is from California, and she did not know anyone here. She has been spending a lot of time with him and his family, but to tell the doctor that I am her father?'* It just did not make sense. He didn't know how to tell his family what Tom had told him.

Sue Jacobs arrived with the file on Caroline. She said that Caroline's parents were both dead, that it did not appear that she had any other family. She had left "next of kin" blank. Richard thanked Sue, and she went over to talk to Donna. The doctor came into the waiting room, asked for Richard and told him that Caroline was out of surgery, things had gone reasonably well but she was still in critical condition, although they were hopeful for a full recovery. She was not conscious yet, but they could just see her for just a minute. Musing to himself, *'Isn't that always what doctors have to say to the grieving family?'* Richard went over to his family and gave them the news. He asked Donna to take Michelle and Doug home in Doug's car, and he would be home shortly. Donna gave Richard a look that was full of questions. She did not ask Richard anything, though. She knew that Richard would tell her when he felt the time was right. Caroline's condition was the priority now.

His emotions stretched taut, Richard went into see Caroline. He was shocked at what he saw. She had a huge bandage on her head, and oxygen tubes and IV tubes and she looked so small and frail. She really had been like part of their family the last six months. She seemed to believe in everything he stood for. She seemed to want to be just like him. He was her mentor. Maybe she did think of him as a father figure, especially since her own parents were dead. *'Poor kid',* he thought. He sat with her for about half an hour. He talked softly to her, telling himself as much as her that everything would be okay. He spoke to her like a father. Maybe she could hear him, maybe that would help her to get well.

"Daddy is here, Caroline. It's going to be okay. We will take care of you. You just need to be strong, and fight to get well." Richard felt like he was choking on his emotions; he had a visceral need to say something more comforting.

She looked so pale and tiny lying there. He hated to leave her, but he need to get some sleep. He would be back in the morning. Michael Wilson's girlfriend, Caroline's nurse, was watching and listening to this intensely personal dialogue.

Richard walked out of her hospital room, and there was Doug, his eyes begging his father for good news.

"Doug, I thought you were going home with your mother and sister, why are you still here?"

Doug just looked at him. "It's all my fault Dad. Is she going to be okay? Is there anything I can do?" The effects of the alcohol had not yet completely left him, despite the intensity of the situation.

Richard put his arm across Doug's shoulders. "Why don't you go in and talk to her?" Doug pulled away, a look of pain crossing his face. "She doesn't want to see me, Dad! The reason she is in here is because of me! She was running away from *me*! She just has to get through this Dad, she just HAS to!"

"Come on, son," Richard said quietly, "let's go home. Things will look better in the morning."

They headed out of the hospital, only to run into a mob of reporters snapping pictures and shouting questions.

"How is your daughter, Governor?" "What happened to make her run out into the street?" Richard was stunned by this sudden appearance of the press. *'How could they know? How had this happened so fast?'* His thoughts raced as he composed himself.

Richard stopped and addressed the reporters. "The girl in the accident is not my daughter. Her name is Caroline Hoffman, and

36

she is a member of my campaign staff."

Michael Wilson stepped up and said "I know for a fact that Caroline Hoffman said she was your daughter. Maybe it is not your daughter, Michelle Johnson, but she *is* claiming to be your daughter. What do you have to say?"

Richard took a calming deep breath, looked at him, and said, "I already told you, she is not my daughter, she works for my campaign. She is also a close friend of our family. Now if you will excuse me, I have no further comment tonight." He and Doug pushed their way through the reporters and over to their car.

When they got into the car, Doug asked Richard, "What was all that about Caroline being your daughter, Dad?"

Richard answered, "Apparently, when Caroline was admitted to the hospital, she regained consciousness for a short time and asked for her dad. She told the doctor that I was her dad. It seems strange, but she does have a head injury, and Sue says that Caroline's parents are both dead. She must think of me like a father."

Doug got a strange look on his face and said, "Dad, I did not even think about this before, but when I kissed Caroline at the club, she screamed out that she was my sister, and that was when she ran out of the club. That's pretty weird that she would say that you are her father and that she's my sister."

Doug was beginning to sober up. "What do you know about her, Dad? What if she has mental problems? She is working on your campaign. Didn't Sue do a background check on her?"

"Now Doug," said Richard sternly, father to son, "don't go jumping to any conclusions here. She is lying in the hospital with a head injury! I'm sure she is just lonely since her parents died, and she has kind of "adopted" us as her family. Besides, Sue ran a full background check on her before we hired her. There was nothing about her that would have been a red flag."

"Dad, she said she was my sister *before* she was injured! I just don't like it. I really think you should look more deeply into her background, seriously." Doug spoke with an intensity that left

Richard unsettled.

Richard started the car, and both men were silent on the ride home deep in thought.

Michael Wilson watched Richard and Doug leave, then pulled out his cell phone, dialing furiously. *'So smug and self-righteous!'* Michael's thoughts were bordering on rage as a voice answered his phone, "You have something for me?"

"You're gonna owe me big time for this one." Michael tried to sound confident. "A young woman was just brought into Harborview Medical Center claiming to be Richard Johnson's daughter. Funny thing is, it wasn't Michelle that was brought in, it was one of Johnson's campaign staffers."

There was silence on the other end for a moment. Quinn Flannery quietly replied as if talking to himself and not Michael, "Gotcha, you self-righteous bastard. I finally got you."

Chapter 4

Who is Caroline?

When they got home, Donna and Michelle were already asleep.

Richard said to Doug, "I guess we better try to get a couple of hours of sleep tonight, if we can. I'll see you in the morning."

"Alright, goodnight Dad," Doug mumbled, and headed up the stairs to his room.

Richard walked around downstairs, checking the doors and windows as he did every night, but his mind was not really on what he was doing. He was thinking about the reporters and what kind of story they might try to make of this. This certainly would have a negative effect on his campaign. This was absolutely not the time for this to have happened. He was very quiet as he got ready for bed so he would not wake Donna. He would tell her everything in the morning. Richard then lay down on the bed and started to think about how he met Caroline.

Six months ago Richard sat in his office thinking about the planning needed to run for the Democratic nomination for the Presidency. His personal pollsters had run the numbers; it seemed likely he had a great shot at being nominated. His thoughts were interrupted when his Campaign Manager, Sue, came into his office with a beautiful young girl and introduced her.

Susan said, "Richard Johnson, this is Caroline Hoffman. She has been calling me for the last six months about wanting to be a volunteer for us. She's from California, and attending Law School at Stanford University, the same school that you got your law degree from. She's heard a lot about you, and decided she wanted to help us."

Richard looked at Caroline and got up and shook her hand. He offered her a seat and said, "So, Caroline, tell me about yourself. I know you are from California. Where in California? Were you born there?"

"Yes sir, I was born only a mile from Stanford University," Caroline answered.

"What made you decide to go into law? Are your parents Democrats?" Richard asked. "And you can dispense with the 'sir'; call me Richard. We don't stand on formality around here." He smiled at her as he spoke.

"Thank you Richard." Caroline went on, "I don't know, my father died when I was six years old. My mother was a hard-line Democrat, though. She encouraged me to go into law. She said a lot of good things about you."

She looked a little nervous as she spoke, but it was like a job interview to her, so that made sense. She was wearing a very conservative, navy blue suit with her hair pulled back, making her seem a little older than she was.

"So are you planning on getting into politics after you get your law degree?" Richard asked.

"I haven't thought that far ahead. That's why I'm here, to learn more about it." Caroline answered.

"Which area were you looking to work on in our campaign?" asked Richard.

"I feel that one of my strengths is being good at handling people, and I would like to work close to you, and help you, but I would be willing to do anything that needs to be done." said Caroline.

"How about answering all of my letters, and organizing my schedule?" suggested Richard.

"That sounds great to me!" said Caroline, sounding both excited and relieved.

Richard suggested to Sue that she work on checking Caroline's background and if nothing negative was found, that she could start as soon as the check was complete. Sue took Caroline to her office and had her fill out her application.

A couple days later, Sue informed Caroline that she had passed her background check and everything was ready for her to start working with the campaign.

The next day Caroline started working with Richard. Always enthusiastic and pleasant, with a big smile on her face, she did a fantastic job of scheduling his meetings and replying to the letters from his supporters. As time went on she was spending more and more time with Richard.

The other people working on the campaign staff began to treat Caroline differently. They had been very nice to her at first, but now they were treating her coldly. They did not feel comfortable with her relationship with Richard. She seemed to be getting too close, and there was some gossip going around the headquarters that the relationship may be inappropriate. Richard's campaign manager, Sue, knew nothing was going on, but she was also aware of the talk. This could not be good for his reputation. Sue had gone to Richard and suggested that Caroline be transferred to a different job position. He had rejected this request, explaining to Sue that he felt comfortable with the job Caroline was doing, and that he really liked her opinion on matters. She was able to give a viewpoint from the younger generation of voters, and anyway, he really liked her. In Richard's opinion, Caroline had a lot to offer his campaign.

While working with Caroline, he got the feeling she was lonely. He decided to introduce her to his family. Maybe his kids would introduce her to some people her age. He talked this idea over with Donna who also agreed it was a great idea. She told Richard to invite her over for that weekend and started planning the meal right away. Not knowing Caroline's likes and dislikes, she decided on lasagna. She had never met anyone that did not like her lasagna. She would make a nice tossed salad and garlic bread to go with it. This was a make-ahead meal, so they would have time to talk and get to know each other. She would serve it out on the porch if the weather were agreeable.

Caroline was so excited about meeting Richard's family. She took forever getting ready. She tried on many different outfits before she could decide on which one to wear. She finally chose a black halter dress with a lilac print all over it. The hemline came to just above her knees, and the fit was perfect. She wore black nylons and black high-heeled sandals. She had planned on wearing her hair down, but she just could not get it to look right, so she put it up with the loose curls falling down. She was pleased with her appearance. She usually took the bus everywhere, but tonight she splurged on a cab. This was a pretty special night for her.

She gave the driver the address, and she was on her way. She held a lovely bunch of tulips on her lap. She hoped Mrs. Johnson liked tulips. The driver pulled up to a gorgeous, gigantic older home with a wrap-around porch. The yard was perfect, flowers everywhere, and not a blade of grass out of place. It sat overlooking Lake Washington, and as she looked around a sense of peace enveloped her. She got out, paid the driver, and started up the walkway. She had butterflies the size of sparrows in her stomach. What if they did not like her? She hoped she would not do anything foolish like spill something or break something. She knew Richard had a son and a daughter, both around her age, but she did not know much about them. She approached the door and thought to herself, '*Well, here I go!*' then knocked on the big wooden door. Richard's wife soon opened the door. Caroline had seen her picture on TV and in the newspaper many times, so she recognized her right away.

"Mrs. Johnson? I am Caroline Hoffman. It is nice to meet you." Caroline handed her the tulips.

Accepting the tulips with a graciousness befitting a politician's wife, Donna replied, "Come on in Caroline, I am happy to meet you too! Richard has told us so much about you! He just thinks the world of you. Please, call me Donna, won't you?" She reached over and gave Caroline a big hug. "Thank you for these beautiful flowers! I just love tulips! Come on in the kitchen with me while I put these in water."

Caroline looked around as she walked through the house. The floors were hardwood, and they just gleamed. There was a huge old curved staircase, and off to the left, was what must be the living room. She followed Donna down a hall and into the most cheerful kitchen she had ever seen. The counters and cupboards and appliances were all white, and the curtains and tablecloth and cushions were all in yellow gingham. This was not at all how she pictured Richard Johnson's kitchen. It was kind of old fashioned and "homey," not sleek and modern like she had thought it would be. It had windows everywhere with a view of the lake from every one.

"I hope you like lasagna, Caroline," Donna said, "I wasn't sure what to fix for dinner."

"I love lasagna!" answered Caroline, looking around the kitchen. "What a cheerful room, did you decorate it?"

"Thank you! Yes, I did. Gingham is a little old fashioned, I know, but it always feels like sunshine in this room and living in Seattle, we can use any extra sunshine we can get!"

"Can I get you something to drink? I just made a fresh batch of iced tea. I thought we would all sit out on the porch and get to know one another before dinner."

Caroline walked around the counter to where Donna was loading a pitcher of tea and glasses onto a tray. "Iced tea sounds delicious. Can I help you with anything?"

Donna handed her the tray and said, "Thanks, if you would carry this tray, I will take these pretty flowers you brought, so we can enjoy them on the porch."

Donna held the door open so Caroline could pass through, and they walked out onto a huge, wrap-around porch overlooking Lake Washington. There was wicker furniture with pretty flowered cushions, and a hanging swing to match. It was just the place

Caroline would love to be on a warm spring evening.

"If you would like to set the tea tray over here, I'll call Richard and the kids." Donna said.

She set the vase with the tulips in the center of one of the tables.

Donna glanced up. "Oh, here they come." Donna called over, "Doug and Michelle, this is Caroline Hoffman, she brought me these beautiful tulips, aren't they pretty?"

"Yes Mom, they *are* pretty, the flowers *and* Caroline!" said Doug. Doug was in love at first sight.

"Douglas! You'll embarrass her!" chided Donna. "Caroline, you'll have to excuse Doug. I am afraid he is a bit of a flirt."

"A *bit* of one?" laughed Michelle, "A big one is more like it! Hi Caroline, nice to meet you. My dad has said some really nice things about you."

"It is nice to meet both of you too. Richard goes on and on about both of you. You are his pride and joy, I can tell," said Caroline.

Just then Richard came out onto the porch. "Hi Caroline, I see you've met my family. Sorry I wasn't able to get out here until now, I had an urgent phone call from Olympia. Thank goodness for phones and fax machines now that we've moved out of the Governor's mansion and back home for my campaign!"

"That's okay. It has been nice meeting everyone, they have made me feel right at home," said Caroline.

"Boy Dad, you never told us how beautiful Caroline was!" said Doug. "I'd have come to campaign headquarters to volunteer if I'd known!"

"Doug, I told you that is enough! You are going to make Caroline uncomfortable." Donna handed Caroline a glass of iced tea. "Have a seat anywhere, Caroline."

Caroline chose a seat that had a view of the lake. "This must be one of the prettiest places in Seattle, and it's right outside your back door! You must feel very lucky to live here."

Donna handed glasses of tea to everyone else, and then poured a glass for herself. "Yes, we hated to leave to go live in Olympia. It just wasn't the same as here. I am *so* glad to be back here again. Long commute for Richard some days, but well worth it, right Richard?"

"Of course it is. We have had this place since the kids were just little. We have so many wonderful memories. This is the best time of year, what with Donna's garden and all of the boats out on the water."

Richard took a long swallow of tea. "Caroline, you'll have to come boating with us sometime. Would you like that?"

"I would love to! I used to go boating with some of my friends on the weekends in California, and I have missed that. I'll bet your house looks fantastic from out on the lake. It is so beautiful! When the cab pulled up, I was really impressed with how pretty it is, and the landscaping is perfect! So far I have only seen the kitchen and entryway, but the inside looks beautiful as well." Caroline couldn't stop herself from gushing.

"Would you like a tour of it before dinner?" offered Donna. "It will be another hour or so until we sit down to dinner."

"That would be great," said Caroline.

"I'll be your tour guide then," said Doug. "We don't exactly live in the White House, at least not yet anyway, but it is a pretty great house!"

"Thanks Doug," said Donna, "I'll get the lasagna into the oven and the table set while you two roam around. Michelle, can you give me a hand?"

"I should check in with Olympia, and see how things are going," said Richard. "I guess we will all meet back up again at dinner!"

Doug led the way back through the kitchen and down the hall into the room Caroline assumed must be the living room when she had first arrived. It turned out this was the library, and it was as beautiful as the rest of what she had seen of the house so far. It had a burgundy leather overstuffed couch and two matching chairs. The tables were all a dark polished wood. Two of the walls were completely lined with bookshelves filled with books. Windows completely covered one wall, so the room, while decorated in dark colors, was light and bright. The fourth wall had two doors, and a huge stone fireplace with a portrait of Richard and his wife hanging above it.

"The library is used mostly as my dad's study," Doug explained. "I remember when I was a kid, this was where we would come when I was in trouble, and Dad would sit me down on that couch and give me a 'talking to'."

"Was Richard a very strict father? I imagine he was awfully busy with his career, wasn't he?" asked Caroline.

"He wasn't any stricter than other fathers, I suppose," answered Doug. "He didn't believe in spanking, but you certainly knew when you had done something wrong. He knew how to give speeches that would make you shape up! He was busy, as most fathers are, I guess. He couldn't coach my baseball teams or anything, but when he was home he spent a lot of time with us. We would go boating and play catch, and he would take us to the zoo. I used to love to go to the zoo. Why? What was your dad like?"

"I don't really remember much about him. He died when I was six," answered Caroline.

"Oh, sorry, I didn't know." Doug felt bad for having asked.

"That's okay, you couldn't have known," said Caroline. "So do I get to see any more of the house or is that it?"

Doug was glad she had lightened the mood with that jab at him. "Oh, there's a lot more to see, follow me!"

Doug walked out of the room and headed into another room even larger than the last one. This one was definitely the living room. It was decorated all in antiques. There were two matching sofas, upholstered in lovely sage green brocade, with intricately carved legs and arms. There was a wood and glass china cabinet filled with little curios. The tall, narrow windows had heavy sage green draperies. There was a white marble fireplace with a long mantle that had framed photographs along its whole length.

Caroline walked over to look at the pictures. There were pictures of what looked like Doug and Michelle as they were growing up. There were some older, black and white photos of a young boy, and others of a young girl, presumably Richard and Donna when they were children. There was a professional portrait of the four of them, which looked to have been taken about four or five years before. Doug had been talking, but Caroline had been lost in her thoughts and had not heard what he'd been saying. He walked over to where she was standing, looking at her expectantly.

"Did you say something Doug?" asked Caroline. "I'm sorry, I was thinking about how I did not have any pictures of me with my dad, and I'm afraid I did not hear what you said."

"That's okay. I was just telling you about my mom's 'knick-knacks', nothing important. Are you ready for the next room?"

Doug headed out the door. "This is just the guest bedroom, and the pantry and bathroom are down this hall. You'll see the dining room when we sit down to eat, so I guess we can head up to the second floor now. There is my room, Michelle's room, my parent's room, a couple of bathrooms, and the family room upstairs. Oh, and my dad has an office off of their bedroom that used to be used a nursery when we were babies."

They headed up the huge staircase that Caroline had seen when she had first arrived. It was just one of those perfect staircases, like you see in the movies. It curved around, with a thick wood railing that was carved into a fancy curl at the end of it. It was carpeted in a deep wine color, and hanging above it from the entryway ceiling was a gorgeous crystal chandelier. Once upstairs, Doug just motioned to the doors and said, "This is my room, that's Michelle's room." He did take her into Richard and Donnas' room, and it was lovely. It looked out over the lake and had a sitting area off of it that was all windows. This room was furnished in antiques as well, decorated in soft peach tones. Caroline walked over to the sitting area and looked out at the view.

Doug came over and said, "Do you know what? When Michelle and I were kids, we used to take that antique spinning wheel of my Mom's and drag it over to this very spot; I would pretend it was the wheel of a giant ship, and we would look out over the water and steer "the ship" with the spinning wheel. Especially if we were having a rain storm, and the windows on all three sides were just getting pounded with rain. I can still remember that, it was so exciting. My mom would get so mad when she would catch us, and she would go on and on about how this was an antique, not a toy."

Caroline tried to imagine what that would have been like, growing up in this house. She could see how a child would think of this as a ship with windows on all three sides of the sitting area and overlooking the lake as it did.

"It sounds like you and Michelle had a pretty great childhood," said Caroline.

"Yeah, I think so. It was more difficult as a teenager, because we weren't allowed to play pranks or get into mischief that other kids did because it would hurt my dad's career, but all in all, I think it was pretty great," replied Doug. "My dad's office is through this door."

He opened it, and Caroline poked her head in the doorway to take a glimpse waving at Richard who was on the phone. He winked at her, and Doug closed the door.

"Now I will show you the best room in the house," Doug said. "I spend most of my free time in here."

It was a gigantic room. At one end of the room were a pool table, a pinball machine, and various home electronics. The other end had a home theater, very comfortable looking sofa and loveseat, two recliners, and a small kitchenette off to one side with a sink, mini-fridge, microwave, and dishwasher.

"This is the family room," Doug announced with a hint of pride in his voice. "I pretty much talked my parents into installing every one of these high-tech gadgets. What do you think?"

"Looks like a fun place for someone with entirely too much time on their hands," said Caroline.

"You sound just like my dad!" laughed Doug.

"I do?" Caroline asked excitedly.

"Yeah, like a politician with way too much work to do. That is not a compliment so don't sound so happy about it! You are way too young to be trying to model yourself after a politician! Want to play a little foosball?" asked Doug.

"What time is it? We should probably be heading down to dinner, shouldn't we?" asked Caroline. "We don't want to keep your mom waiting."

"You're no fun, you really do sound like my dad." Doug whined, but he started towards the door.

They walked into the dining room, just as Donna was setting the salads on the table. "Perfect timing, kids. Doug, show Caroline where she can freshen up before dinner."

"I just showed her the whole house, Mom, she knows where the bathroom is." said Doug. Michelle walked in, just at that moment.

"Talk about rude Doug, what is wrong with you?" asked Michelle.

"I think he's mad because I wouldn't play foosball with him," laughed Caroline.

"Figures", said Michelle, "Come on Caroline, I'll show you the way."

After they had left the room, Donna turned to Doug. "What's up Doug?"

"For such a babe, she is sure serious, isn't she?" Doug said.

"She is probably just shy; she just met you an hour ago. I'm sure she would love to beat you in a good game of foosball!" Donna said, as she gave him a playful shove towards the kitchen.

"Wash up at the kitchen sink, and sit down to dinner and behave yourself for a change!"

They all sat down to dinner, and Richard said grace. As they started on their salads, Richard asked, "So, Caroline, what do you think of the house?"

"It is just wonderful! It is beautiful and comfortable at the same time. I just love the staircase! It's the kind a girl dreams about walking down in a beautiful long dress, while her prom date waits at the bottom of the staircase looking up at her. Michelle, was it just perfect?" Caroline asked.

"Yeah, isn't that funny that all little girls picture that staircase? It must be from watching Cinderella one too many times, or something. I think I want to hold my wedding here and walk down it in my wedding dress someday," answered Michelle.

"Oh, me too!" said Caroline, and everyone looked at her kind of oddly, and she added "I mean a staircase like that one, someday."

"It is a great staircase," said Donna. "After dinner, I will have to have Michelle take you out and show you my garden. I have worked on it for years, and it is just the way I want it. I think it would be a lovely place to stage a wedding."

"Oh, I would love to see your garden!" said Caroline.

The conversation turned to flowers, the weather, and work. Caroline was impressed with the way they could all joke with one another. She could see they were a loving, caring family. The press had always portrayed them that way, but in this case it was actually the truth. When they were done eating, Caroline offered to help with the dishes. "Nonsense, you are our guest!" replied Donna. "The kids will help me with the dishes."

"Mom, you promised Caroline she could see your garden. Michelle is much better at doing dishes than me. So I'll tell you what. I will continue my tour out into the garden, and Michelle can help you, how about that?" said Doug.

"Yeah right Doug, anything to get out of doing the dishes," said Michelle sarcastically, "but since you started with the house tour, I will let you get out of it this time. You go ahead and take Caroline out to the garden."

"Thanks sis," Doug grinned, "I owe you one!"

"You owe me more than one, you know!" laughed Michelle.

Doug and Caroline walked out to the porch, down the stairs, and towards the side of the house. They went through an archway with gorgeous purple clematis vines growing on it. They stepped into a garden that was absolutely magical. There were rose bushes all around the perimeter, and more roses climbing up trellises behind those. There were hydrangeas, rhododendrons, and lilacs. There was a fountain in the middle with several white wrought iron chairs and benches surrounding it. There were gazing balls, garden fairies, and birdhouses. The walkway going through all of this was cobblestone, and there were raised beds built of cobblestones as well. In the raised beds were flowers of every shape and color, tulips, hyacinths, crocus, iris, carnations, pansies and primroses. Caroline thought she could just stay out here forever.

Doug was quiet for quite awhile, then stepped up beside her and asked in a low voice, "So, what do you think?"

"Oh, Doug, it is just magical!" Caroline answered. "The sight, the sound, and the fragrance... even the feel of the breeze off the water. Wow, this is the best place in Seattle."

"I like to watch people for a few minutes after they come in here. Some of them feel just as you do, that it is a special magical place. Others just see a garden, nothing more. I had a feeling you would think it was special. My mom is so proud of this garden. She has worked out here for years making little changes here and there. I am glad you like it, and she will be, too." Doug said. "Want to have a seat for awhile?" he asked, gesturing at one of the benches.

"Sure, let's sit over here," Caroline answered and picked a bench facing the fountain next to a gazing ball.

They sat in silence for a few minutes, and then Doug asked, "How long have you been in Washington?"

"Almost seven months," answered Caroline.

"Have you seen anything of Seattle, yet?"

"No, I have not had time. I've been working on the campaign."

"You can't work 24 hours a day, seven days a week."

"No, but I have not made any close friends here yet. It's no fun to go out alone."

"No one from the campaign office has asked you out yet?"

Caroline let out a sigh, "No, sometimes I think they don't like me. They only talk to me about work."

"Well, that is hard to believe. How about I take you out on the town and show you the sights? Seattle is a great town. You can't live here for seven months without going to all of the famous places."

"Where would you be taking me?" Caroline asked, looking at him with a mischievous glint in her eyes. Doug found himself more bedeviled than before by her.

"Everywhere! Seattle Center, Pike Place Market, The Waterfront, The Ballard Locks, Safeco Field for a Mariner's baseball game, and Mt. Rainier National Park. Where do you want to go first?"

"How about Seattle Center? I would like to see the Experience Music Project. Who would be going? Do you think Michelle would come with us?"

"Yeah, I guess she probably would. Want to go next Saturday?"

"Sure, that would be great, thanks Doug. It is getting late, we should probably go in now, don't you think?"

They headed back to the house where Richard, Donna and Michelle were sitting on the porch. Richard and Donna were on the swing wrapped together in a blanket. Michelle had an afghan over her shoulders, and Caroline noticed there were blankets draped across the back of two other chairs. As they got to the porch, Richard said, "It gets pretty chilly at night, but the lights on the water are so pretty, we just curl up in a blanket and sit out on the porch anyway. Why don't you two grab some blankets and join us?"

Michelle asked, "So what do you think of my Mom's garden?"

"It is pure magic," answered Caroline, "I could sit in it forever. What a truly special place; it just fills your senses."

"Thank you Caroline," said Donna, "That is exactly how I feel about it."

They chatted for another 30 minutes or so, and Caroline asked if she could use the phone to call a cab. Doug said he would be more than happy to run her home, and she gratefully accepted. They chatted about music most of the way home, and when he dropped her off; he offered to walk her up to her door. She said it was not necessary, as you could see her door from the curb, so he sat in the car until he saw that she was safely in her apartment, and headed back home.

Thinking about how he met Caroline, Richard slowly fell asleep, hoping that all was not lost.

Although it was almost 4 o'clock in the morning, Tom Gibson found himself unable to sleep. He could not believe his luck. Here he had been thinking that Richard Johnson had beat him to the punch yet again, and now the holier-than-thou, perfect family man was facing a scandal of epic proportions on the very night he announces his candidacy. He had to be careful, though. An outright attack on a man of Richard Johnson's stature was not something to be done lightly. No, he decided, I'll let this play out in the press for a few days and see how he responds.

He called Josh and told him to hold off on the O'Reilly interview for a few days. He explained that with what had just happened, he wanted to see how Richard handled himself before he faced his interview. Josh said he would make the appropriate calls and take care of it. With that comforting thought resonating through his head, Tom slipped into a happy slumber.

In DC, Vice-President Newman had just received the news about Caroline's accident as well as the things she had said about Richard being her father. He lay in bed, his wife slumbering next to him, his thoughts racing. These were the times Newman was at his best; when a highly credentialed opponent showed a crack in their armor, he always knew how to attack.

Should the Democratic Party candidate winner be Tom Gibson, Newman was confident that he win Tom with the majority. Richard however was a young, energetic and respected family man. It appeared this was going to be a hard win.

Newman roused himself, throwing on a robe as he headed to his den to call Bill Campbell, his Campaign Manager. He gave Bill some instructions for the coming weeks, laying out his plan to attack Richard using public rallies and the media. Bill agreed with his boss, as always. Sometimes Bill wondered why Newman even bothered with having a Campaign Manager; he always seemed to have more ideas and strategies than his staff.

Chapter 5

The Aftermath

The next day the press filled the airwaves and newspapers with stories of the accident. The Seattle Times-Sentinel proclaimed that Presidential Candidate and Washington State Governor Richard Johnson's daughter had been in an accident, but did not state that it was Michelle. CWWX Radio stated that a girl involved in a car accident was claiming that she was the daughter of Richard Johnson. While the girl was unconscious, Richard had talked to her as if she were his daughter. This was the central theme to all the stories. Who is this girl? Is she Richard's daughter or not? It was an embarrassing situation for the Johnson family. The phones at the campaign office, the Governor's office, and Richard's home were ringing constantly. Some people began to privately and publicly question this man they had always thought to be a moral and upstanding politician.

Despite getting only a few hours of sleep, Richard awoke early that morning to a call from a doctor at the hospital, who informed him that Caroline was still in critical condition and they needed to perform another operation to save her. They needed information and they needed volunteers to donate blood as Caroline had a rare blood type, AB negative. Richard was stunned to hear this; he was also blood type AB negative, which he knew to be rare.

Richard told the doctor that Caroline's parents were dead, and she had no next of kin. He explained that she was a very close friend of their family that she worked for him and he would take full responsibility for any financial arrangements needing to be made for the surgery. His family would be willing to donate blood, and he would try to get more donors from his campaign headquarters. He would bring her personnel file and try to complete any information for them that he could. He would be there just as soon as he was able.

Richard turned on the TV after hanging up with the doctor. He needed to see what kind of political lashing he was in for today before he left for the office. As it happened, the channel was broadcasting Vice-President Newman's speech at a rally of thousands of his supporters. Richard could only watch as Newman pilloried him over the situation with Caroline.

Newman stood as tall as he was able, drinking in the waves of adoration coming from the crowd. He smiled benevolently at them as he began to speak, "What we have here is a so-called family values candidate, who now appears to be the father of an illegitimate child. The girl told the doctors and nurses that Johnson is her father. When Richard Johnson visited her in the hospital he told her quote 'Daddy is here don't worry'. She is also a member of his campaign staff." Newman paused before he thunderously asked the crowd, "Can we trust a person like him to be this country's President?"

The crowd murmured loudly, "No..No." Some shouted their replies. Newman stood taller; he had them in the palm of his hand now. Now was the time to fully reel them in.

He continued, "During his interview with Bill O'Reilly, Johnson wouldn't say if he is for or against abortion. Now we know why! It is because he has an illegitimate child! You all know where *I* stand on abortion. Why is Johnson confused about the beginning of life? A fetus is a life and removing it is the same as murdering it! How can he be confused about this issue? I agree if a woman is raped she has the right to end the life of a fetus, but that is *only* if she takes action during the first trimester." As he said this last statement, he pounded his hands down on the podium.

The crowd responded again thunderously, with clapping and loud yelling and whistling.

Richard could only sit and watch, aghast at what was happening. *Newman and everyone else have been waiting for years for him to make a mistake.* He felt his world slipping away as he continued to watch Newman's speech.

Newman let the applause continue for a moment, then raised his hands so that he could continue his speech.

"What do we think of Johnson's views on gay rights?" The crowd began to boo loudly as Newman continued, "God created man and woman for a reason, otherwise there would be just men or just women. The reason God created man *and* woman is to have children. Can a man and a man produce children? Can a woman and a woman produce children? The answer is NO! Why is he confused? I'll tell you why, he wants to play both sides against the middle. We have seen from his statements on abortion that he will not commit himself one way or another. His policy on gay rights is the same."

The crowd had worked itself into a fervor now. Newman knew he was on the right track; picking Richard apart piece by piece.

"Let me address his foreign policies. If Richard Johnson becomes President, he will lead us all to disaster. If he becomes President he will let terrorists dictate to us how we should act, how we should stay out of other country's affairs. Johnson has no foreign affairs experience that qualifies him to be our Commander-in-Chief. He did not serve in the military; he does *not* know what our soldiers fight and die for. He forgets that this country was built by people who were *not* afraid of other countries and did *not* allow themselves to be told what to do or how to live. *I* will provide security for this country; *I* will not allow terrorists nor any other country to tell *us* how to live!"

At this, Newman raised his hands above his head to the overwhelming applause and support he could feel from the crowd.

He roared, "If you elect me, I will lead this country back to the greatness that it rightly deserves!"

Tom Gibson was intently absorbing Newman's words and processing the side benefits for himself, "Finally the break I've been waiting for" he muttered to himself, "I'll use both Newman's theme and words to get Johnson out."

Richard flipped off the TV and sat back on the bed. Donna had been awakened by the volume of the TV and had watched Newman's speech in silence. Now she sat up in bed and moved next to Richard, whispering, "Don't you let him get to you Richard Johnson. This situation has not fully been explained by anyone yet."

Richard gave her a squeeze, then rose to shower and dress and head for the office.

Richard rushed to Campaign headquarters, only to be mobbed by the media. He made his way through, stating, "No comment." He headed straight to Sue's office.

Sue was frantically pacing when she saw him enter. "Richard this is going to get a lot worse before it gets better. What is going on? Think! Have you ever had an affair?" She needed to ask the questions. It was time to move to damage control mode.

Richard vehemently responded, "NO! Sue, I can't believe you just asked me that! I have NEVER been unfaithful to Donna! We've been married over 26 years! I love her deeply, and would never even consider it! Caroline Hoffman is NOT my daughter, she is just a confused mixed-up kid, lying in a hospital bed and fighting for her life. Someone has got to help her!"

Richard paused as he ran his fingers through his hair. He stared out his office window into the darkness. Turning again to Sue, he spoke, his emotions under control for the moment.

"I want a memo sent around letting everyone at campaign headquarters know that we need blood donors who have AB negative blood. I need Caroline's personnel file right away. I'm taking it with me to the hospital. Let's get Caroline all the help she needs, and then we will worry about cleaning up this political mess. What is more important, someone's life, or someone's career?"

"Richard, I'm sorry. Of course you're right, I have her file right here. Take the back way out to avoid the press. My car is parked out back, so let's exchange keys and you can take my car. I will drive yours to the hospital, and we can switch back later. I'll leave for the hospital after you get out of the parking lot. Please forgive me for doubting you."

"It's okay, Sue. I know you're just concerned about my career. It's your career on the line, too. After all the years we've worked together I know I can trust you and I know you have to ask these questions. At the moment, I just want to make sure Caroline makes it through this. Once she recovers, she can set the story straight, and everything will be okay. It will take some work, but I am confident we can repair the damage this is doing."

Richard rushed to the hospital; as he pulled up he could see reporters waiting for him to appear there. As soon as he walked in, the press surrounded him. Questions were flying all around him.

"Governor, is that your daughter or not?" "Why are you closer to her than you are to your other campaign workers?" "Are you donating blood?" "Why are you paying for her medical expenses?" The flood of questions was difficult to comprehend. Richard had never dealt with the press being so militant before.

Richard pushed his way through the crowd, avoiding all of them, saying nothing. Just in front of the door, blocking his way was Michael Wilson and his cameraman.

Michael asked, "Isn't it possible that she is your daughter?"

Richard said, "No, it isn't, please move out of my way."

"Yesterday when she was unconscious you were heard saying to her, and I quote, 'Your dad will take care of you.' Why did you say that if she is not your daughter?" Richard did not respond and kept walking.

"Isn't it true that she was born and raised near Stanford University, and you lived there the years before and after she was born?"

"Your statements are all true, but she is not my daughter. That's all I can tell you. Excuse me please."

"Couldn't she be the result of an affair you had with her mother?"

Richard was mad now. "No! I told you she is not my daughter! I have never had an affair. Now get out of my way!"

At this, Michael stepped out of his way. Richard knew that Sue was not going to be happy about that. He knew enough about Michael Wilson to know that he would not let up that easily when he smelled a story. He had to get into the hospital. This was not looking good for him. He headed straight for the admissions office to find out what help he could give on the paperwork for Caroline. He then headed down to the lab to have a blood test performed. Following the test he found a chair in the waiting room and sat down to await the results.

The doctors came in a few minutes later. Tests showed that Richard's blood type was a match, as he knew it would, so he headed back to the lab to give blood.

He asked if he could see Caroline before she went in for surgery, and they told him he could, for just a few minutes. When he went in, she was in bad shape. Caroline kept looking at him but was unable to say anything. Richard tried to say with his eyes that everything was going to be fine, just in case she was unable to hear his words. *'This surgery would fix her right up, and she would be as good as new. She was semi-conscious, of course, but one never knew. Maybe she could hear him. Maybe it would help. Please God, let this help!'* He dropped a kiss on her forehead, and quietly left the room.

Outside, the doctor who would be performing the surgery explained that after the operation, Caroline would be put into an induced coma to allow her to heal. The doctor went on to explain that Caroline had a blood clot in her brain that was threatening her very survival. The operation would take several hours, so the doctor advised him to find a place to wait and he would inform Richard as soon as possible of the results.

Sue was also waiting for him in the hall. She had seen the newscasts showing his outburst with Michael Wilson. She was not happy with him to say the least. She asked about Caroline's condition. He told Sue that his blood type was a match, and she would be taken to surgery soon. Sue asked Richard to promise her he would not say anything to any member of the media until after Caroline recovered, and then they could clear this all up. If she did not recover, they would deal with that when and if the time came. He agreed to her request. They exchanged car keys, and he decided to head home and wait there for news on Caroline. There was nothing he could do here, and he needed to speak with his family.

A thought occurred to Richard as he was leaving. Turning to Sue, he quietly instructed her to get in touch with the Secret Service office and request some protection for his family and for Caroline. As a formal Presidential candidate, he knew they had to respond to his request. He did not want to take this action, but he needed to know that he and his family would be safe until this situation resolved itself. Sue said she would take care of it immediately.

Chapter 6

Family Reaction

When he got home, there were reporters camped out on the street in front of his house. He just drove right on by, thankful for garage door openers and attached garages. He went upstairs, and Donna, Michelle, and Doug were all in the family room, watching the news. They got up when he walked in.

"Dad, they're saying that you had an affair, and that Caroline is your daughter," said Michelle. "Doug says that she told him she was his sister. What is going on?"

"Michelle, honey, Caroline is not my daughter. I have never been with anyone except for your mother, I swear. *No one.* Your mother and I were high school sweethearts, and I have never been unfaithful to her in my life. I do not know what is going on. We need Caroline to regain consciousness to help us figure this all out, which won't happen anytime soon. Her operation is going to take several hours and the doctor said she will be put into a coma afterward to allow her to heal more quickly. This has been blown all out of proportion because I am a Presidential candidate, and the media is trying to come up with a scandal that is just not there. I am very sorry we all have to go through this, but you will just have to believe me, I have never cheated on your mother, not even once."

"I believe you Dad, I never thought you did. This is all just so crazy!" Michelle ran over and gave him a big hug.

"Dad how is Caroline?" asked Doug, looking exhausted. "Is she going to be okay?" Doug was fighting the effects of a nasty hangover.

"Doug, she is in surgery right now. We can only pray, and let God take care of her. She has some of the best doctors in the world working on her, son."

"Kids, can I talk to your mom for a little bit?" Richard asked.

Doug and Michelle nodded and got up, leaving Richard and Donna alone.

Richard walked over and gathered Donna into his arms.

"Donna, I am *so* sorry this is happening sweetheart. I do not know why it is. I'm afraid for our future, and I imagine you're questioning our past, and I don't blame you if you are having some doubts. All I can do is reassure you that I have *never* been unfaithful to you. You are the only woman I have ever been with, and the only woman I will ever want. You are everything to me. You are all that I need. I hate that this is hurting you. I have gone over it in my mind time and time again, and there is simply no explanation. The only thing I could even come up with is if I had donated to a sperm bank, but I never have. I do not know why our blood types match up. Do you have any questions that I haven't answered?" He tried to meet her eyes, but couldn't.

"Doug thinks she is maybe doing this on purpose to hurt you or your campaign. He says that she claimed to be his sister before she was hurt. Why would she come all the way from California to work on your campaign unless she had an ulterior motive?" asked Donna. "Did you give any thought to that? Possibly you made an enemy at college that you are unaware of, and they paid her to come here and work for you, maybe a political enemy. You know that Flannery and especially Newman would love nothing better than to sabotage this campaign. You've been at each other's throats for years now."

She paused, "I know being hit was an accident, but she *is* the one who told the doctors that you were her father. Maybe you should have a DNA test to prove her wrong."

Richard sighed, "Let's see if she regains consciousness, and has a good explanation. If she does not, then I will do the test,

I promise, okay? I also asked Sue to get in touch with the Secret Service for some protection. I didn't want to resort to that, but I need to know that you are all safe."

Donna replied, "All right, we can wait and see what she has to say. As for the protection, do what you think you need to; we'll deal with it. I really do not feel like cooking. Do you think Jeremy and Kevin would bring a couple of pizzas by? I think Doug needs his friends right now anyway. I think I'll have Michelle call them and ask. Do you have any cash on you to pay them back? Those reporters are an absolute nuisance, and the telephone is ringing continuously."

Richard was relieved to talk about something else besides Caroline. "Good idea, I think I have some money on me. Doug really feels this is his fault, poor guy. I'm sure they would be happy to help out a friend."

An hour later, Jeremy and Kevin arrived with dinner. Michelle had been watching for their car, and opened the garage for them as they pulled in. Michelle had not pulled her car in the garage, so there was an empty stall. Doug was in the family room, so the guys left a pizza in the kitchen for Richard and Donna and Michelle, and took the other one upstairs. When they walked into the family room, Doug was lying on the couch, staring at the ceiling.

"Hey Doug, what's up?" asked Kevin. "We brought you some pizza."

"Doug, you know it is not your fault that Caroline was hit by that car." said Jeremy. "You can't be blaming yourself, man. You've liked Caroline for so long, I'm surprised you took this long to make a move. All you did was try to kiss her. That happens all the time. You were in a public place. It's not like she felt trapped, or in any danger or anything. She shouldn't have run clear out into the street. She could have run to the bathroom, or just gone back to the table. You can't take the blame for her accident Doug. It was an accident, plain and simple, it could have happened to anyone."

Just then Richard entered the room. "Doug, I just got a call from the hospital. The surgery went well, but Caroline won't be conscious until they feel the time is right. Just thought I would let you know the good news."

"Thanks Dad." Doug said, "I'm glad the surgery went well."

Richard went back downstairs, leaving Doug's friends to cheer him up.

"Well there you go Doug. It sounds like Caroline is going to be fine. Now get over here and have a piece of pizza. By tomorrow morning you will be visiting her at the hospital, and she can tell you herself that this is totally not your fault!" exhorted Jeremy.

Doug got up off of the couch and grabbed a piece of pizza, but he wasn't hungry. His friends didn't know yet what Caroline had said, both to him and to his father. He'd just as soon leave it that way for now. He just picked at the toppings, but it got Jeremy off of his back.

"Hey Doug, how about a game of foosball?" asked Jeremy. "Why don't you and Kevin play, I'm really not in the mood," answered Doug. "Doug, you are going to get Michelle mad at us. She asked us to come over and cheer you up, and you are *not* cooperating with us! Kevin is scared to death of your sister, you know that. You have to at least *act* like we cheered you up so he won't have to deal with "the wrath of Michelle!" laughed Jeremy.

"You guys, I am not afraid of her, I just don't like it when she gets ticked at us for something!" Kevin replied petulantly. "Come on Doug; let me kick your butt at the foosball table."

"Okay, fine. I'll play, if it will get you guys to shut up!" said Doug as he headed over to the table.

Michelle came in as they were playing, and whispered 'thanks' to Jeremy, and he winked at her. He knew how much she cared about her brother, even though she would never admit it to anyone. Kevin won the foosball game, and Doug told Michelle that they had agreed the winner would have to play Michelle.

"No way, we never agreed," started Kevin, but Jeremy cut him off.

"Oh come on Kevin, we did too. You won, and now you have to play Michelle!" Jeremy laughed. "Go on, Michelle; show him how it's done!"

The rest of the afternoon went well. They managed to keep Doug's spirits up. Kevin and Jeremy left at around eleven-thirty. They were glad they were able to help out their friend.

Richard was aware that Tom Gibson was traveling all over the states and pushing his campaign. Newman's speech was resonating well with people and he realized that as a candidate he needed to be proactive before the situation spiraled out of control.

Downstairs, when he heard everyone retire for the night, Richard made a phone call.

This call was one of the most painful things he had ever done, but he had worked too long and hard to let this situation ruin his career and the well being of his family. If he had to swallow his pride to get things back on track, so be it. The conversation was short; whether it was effective or not only time would tell.

As Richard hung up the phone, he couldn't help but reflect on the old adage 'keep your friends close, your enemies closer. Have I done the right thing?' Political infighting and brokering deals to get what you wanted or needed was familiar to him in the political arena, but he much preferred to be face to face with someone. He had made his reputation as a fair but firm straight dealer. He wasn't feeling very comfortable with this kind of subterfuge.

Chapter 7

Trust

The next morning, on his way to the hospital, Richard stopped by the campaign office. He had called the hospital before he left, and Caroline's condition had not changed since the night before. He headed straight for Sue's office. He could see by the look on her face that something was wrong.

"What is it, Sue, what's happened?"

Sue replied, "Tom Gibson and Republicans are using the word TRUST, namely your loss of trust with the public. They're calling you a fraud. Some of our Democratic supporters have been calling me and asking me to clear up the problem or." Sue trailed off for a moment then sighed heavily and went on. "Tom Gibson is flying high. He is everywhere campaigning and using Trust as his key word.

"Can you Trust Richard Johnson now?

"The latest polls show we are losing support, and that means we will be losing funds. CNBR's latest results have you down to 45% support of your candidacy in the next primary and caucuses states. No money has come in since this happened. You know end of the primaries and caucuses are not too far away? Have the doctors given you any indication of when Caroline might regain consciousness? Every hour is crucial to this campaign. We have got to clear up this mystery. It is hurting us with every passing hour, Richard."

Sue looked really worried. "I think you should have a DNA

test done, and the sooner the better."

"Yeah, Donna has suggested that too." replied Richard, running his fingers through his hair. "I wanted to give Caroline a chance to explain first, but it is going to take longer than I thought for her to wake up. Go ahead and look into the testing Sue. I'm going to head over to the hospital now and sit with Caroline for a while. Call me if you need me for anything. I'm really sorry about all of this, but I just know there is a logical explanation."

Richard had to wade through reporters at the entrance to the hospital. He managed to get past them without saying a word, as Sue had asked of him. This was really becoming a nightmare. He just wished Caroline would wake up. He was glad to see a guard posted at her door. *'The Secret Service doesn't waste any time, do they!'* But the sight of the guard reassured Richard immensely. He could just see that reporter, Michael Wilson, weaseling his way in and trying to wake her up to get a story. He stopped and spoke with the nurse on duty on his way past the nurse's station.

"Any change?"

"None, sir. I'm sorry. We all are," the nurse replied.

He was getting tired of that answer every time he asked how Caroline was. As he entered Caroline's room, he noticed several new bouquets of fresh flowers. He walked around, and read the cards. Several people from the campaign office had sent some, and one was from Kevin, Jeremy and Beth. *'That was nice of them'*, Richard thought. Caroline seemed to have quite a few friends, but nothing from any relatives. Richard knew every one of the people that had sent flowers. If all of these people thought enough of Caroline to send her flowers, then how could she possibly be the kind of person that would deliberately sabotage someone's campaign? No, he did not believe that. There just had to be another answer. He walked over to sit at her bedside, and began to talk quietly to her.

"Your surgery went well yesterday. It turns out you and I have the same rare blood type. Did you know that? You have some really nice flower arrangements here, one is made of yellow roses, and one has several shades of purple. The one by your window is multi-colored. They really brighten the place up, you should try opening your eyes and see for yourself."

She did not move at all. He was half-hoping she would just open up her eyes and look around. *'Wishful thinking, I guess.'*

He had checked in at campaign headquarters, and Sue seemed to have things under control as much as she could under the circumstances. He had called in to Olympia from his cell phone on the ride to the hospital, and the Lieutenant Governor, while upset with the bad press, seemed to be handling things there. Caroline was sleeping peacefully, and Doug and Michelle's friends seemed to be helping them out which left just one more person. He was worried about Donna, the most important person to him. He knew he better get home and see what he could do to help her. He left Caroline's room and headed for his car.

As he approached the exit to the parking lot, he could see the mob of press still waiting for him. He decided to take a few minutes and respond as well as he could, otherwise they wouldn't let him through.

Reporters and TV crews ran towards Richard as he exited the hospital. He stopped and told them that he would speak for a few minutes, then he would need to get home and see to his family. He pointed at one reporter.

The reporter quickly told his cameraman to focus on Richard, then asked, "Governor Johnson, what's your response to Tom Gibson and Vice-President Newman' comments about your stand on abortion? Do you agree with his statement that you aren't clear on this issue?

Richard replied, "Do *you* know when life begins? I certainly don't and have never pretended to know. If life begins as a fetus, why aren't we issuing death certificates for miscarriages? People who care about abortions should first take care of the homeless, the poor single mothers and their children. Every woman has the right to provide for her own welfare. Who has the power to tell a raped or sick or dying mother to have her child? These issues have to be understood and evaluated on their own merit. Don't take me wrong, abortion as a means of birth control is wrong, no question about it, but can we force it on a woman without understanding her individual situation?"

The nurse who broke the story to Michael Wilson was watching and, catching Wilson's eye, gave him a thumbs-up, encouraging him to ask the next question.

Richard looked at Wilson and pointed to him.

Wilson asked, "Governor, I understand that your blood is compatible with Caroline's. She has a rare blood type. Why is it that you match?"

Richard knew this would be difficult to explain; given the rarity of the blood type and the statistical probability of Caroline's blood matching.

"I care about people and gave blood to help save the girl. Yes, my blood type is AB negative and hers is the same. There is nothing more to this than coincidence. Now, excuse me please. I have nothing more to say."

Richard made his way through the mob of reporters, once again, and headed home. This was supposed to be one of the happiest and most exciting times of their lives. Instead it was the worst. Why was this happening to them? Things were going so great just a few short days ago. Soon he was maneuvering his way through another crowd of reporters gathered at his gate. Well, at least one more thing he could be thankful for were automatic gates. He pulled into the garage and went into the house.

Chapter 8

Why Should I Trust Him?

After being introduced to the pair of Secret Service agents assigned to the house, Richard went to find his wife. He found Donna on the porch staring out at the lake. He could tell right away that she was upset. He walked over to her, and laid his cheek on the top of her head. Usually when he did this, she would turn his face up to his for a kiss. Today, she did not move.

"I saw the outburst you had last night with Michael Wilson on the news again this morning. They say support for your campaign is slipping because of this whole mess. It was right to go to the hospital the night of the accident because our son was with her at the time, and she worked for you, but I think you are making it worse by showing up there every couple of hours to donate blood. I think we need to distance ourselves from her until we know what the true story is. She could be trying to ruin your chances at becoming President. You can't know for sure! What happens if she never regains consciousness? You shouldn't say she is like a daughter to us. That makes it sound like you are confirming her story that she is your daughter."

Donna stood. "I am going to go sit in my garden for a while. I would appreciate it if you would leave me alone for the time being." With that she got up and walked away from Richard and into the garden.

Richard was astounded. Donna knew him better than anyone. They had been high school sweethearts, and now she doubted him.

He felt like the bottom had just dropped out of his world. He sat down in the chair that Donna had just vacated to do some thinking himself.

Donna sat down on her favorite bench in front of the fountain. She loved Richard as much as she ever had, and deep down, she knew he would never have been unfaithful to her. But this was hard to swallow. She couldn't shake the guilt that she felt over doubting her husband; he had never really let her down before. She let her memory take her back to when she and Richard first met and fell in love over 29 years ago…

It was a very sunny day in July, and Donna was only sixteen years old. She was enrolled in swimming classes at her high school. Richard was a lifeguard at her school's pool. He had volunteered for the job. He was a very strong swimmer and being a volunteer looked good on his college transcripts. The first time Donna saw Richard, he had flashed her that gorgeous smile of his. He had a wonderful tan contrasted by his white teeth and curly auburn hair. She remembered how she had felt butterflies in her stomach every time Richard even looked at her. One day while she was swimming in the deep end of the pool, she got a terrible cramp in her leg and could not swim. She cried out, and Richard dove into the pool putting an arm around her and getting her safely out of the pool. That was when he had first asked her out.

He had taken her to a drive-in movie. She did not remember what movie it was. She had been so anxious to make a good impression. All she thought about had been her hair and her makeup and making sure she did not say the wrong thing or spill anything. She must have done okay though because at the end of the evening he had asked her for a second date. From that day on, they had been together every day.

Their parents soon became friends, and everyone just naturally assumed they would someday be married. Richard completed his BA at the University of Washington a year later, and Donna graduated from high school. They both applied to Stanford

University, Richard for Law School and Donna for Business Management, and both had been accepted. They had rented an apartment near the University and lived together for three years before deciding to get married.

They flew back to Seattle for the wedding, and it was magnificent. Richard's parents had the most wonderful back yard, with lilac bushes all around it. It smelled just like heaven and was the most perfect setting for their wedding. As was the fad back in those days, Donna had worn a wreath of fresh flowers in her hair, instead of a veil, and a beautiful, yet simple, long white satin dress. She remembered how happy she had been that day. Richard had made her happy every day since then. Donna could not think of a day when Richard had ever been away from her. He was the best husband, best father, best person she had ever known.

How could this be happening? What could possibly be the explanation? Then she remembered the time her dad had been terribly ill, and she had flown back to help her mom out for a week. It had been before they had had children, but how long before? Was it at all possible that Richard could have had an affair the *one* week she had *ever* been away from him? She wished she could remember just exactly when that had been...

'Donna, quit doubting your husband, for goodness sake! You know he has been just as faithful as you have been; shame on you! You've known him for almost 30 years!' She thought to herself.

She walked over to a lilac bush, and breathed in the fragrant scent. It took her back to her wedding day and reminded her of how much she had loved, and still loved her husband. She almost ran to the porch and over to where Richard was sitting, and sat right down on his lap and gave him a big bear hug.

"I love you Richard Johnson, and whatever happens, we will get through it together."

"I love you too, Donna, more than you could ever know. I am going to see about that DNA test right now. This is not fair to you, the kids, or the campaign staff. I can't put the feelings of *one* girl ahead of the feelings of so many of the people that I care about. You are upset, Sue is really stressed out, as are the rest of the campaign staff, I imagine. The kids can't even leave their own house without the press hounding them. Enough is enough. I am sorry I did not agree to it right away."

As Richard held Donna, he thought back to last night's phone call and hoped that it would be enough.

Tom Gibson reflected on all the press that Richard had gotten since this situation had happened. He was in the driver's seat, although he had his doubts that he could defeat Vice-President Newman. If Richard was considered a newcomer to the national stage, Tom Gibson was even more unknown outside of the State of Washington. But Tom Gibson was no spring chicken, either. He had to make a move now or time was going to pass him by. Newman was a formidable opponent, but so, Gibson mused, was he. If Richard's campaign failed, he would be waiting to step into the void.

Chapter 9

Family Fallout

Doug had slipped out of the house while his parents were discussing the situation. He could tell that they needed their privacy, so he had slipped out the back, and accompanied by a Secret Service agent, drove to the mall. He had thought that no one would recognize him, the accident had only happened a few days ago after all. He was wrong.

As he browsed the shops in the mall, he heard a voice yell out, "Hey, aren't you Johnson's son?"

Doug looked around to spot the source of the voice and saw an older man approaching him. The agent moved closer to Doug, asking him if he wanted the man removed.

Doug replied, "No, he doesn't look dangerous. Let him come."

The man walked up to Doug and began to angrily speak at Doug.

"Your father has let us all down! I believed in him and his family-first talk and now this happens!"

Doug attempted to answer, but the man cut him off, continuing to work himself up.

"Your dad is a fraud! I will *not* vote for him, neither should anyone else, if they're smart!" His voice rose in tone. "Why should I believe a word he says now? Huh? Tell me!"

The man's voice was attracting attention, and passersby began to stop and gather around him. Doug could see that this was not going to be resolved here.

"Sir, my father is an honorable man. I believe in him and nothing is going to change that!" Doug started to turn away, but the man grabbed him by the arm. The agent grabbed the man's other arm and took him to the ground. The situation was on the verge of being another incident that would look bad for his father's campaign.

Doug told the agent to let the man up. The agent complied immediately, helping the man to his feet.

Doug apologized to the man, who walked off still angry. Doug watched him leave, then stated to the crowd, "There's nothing more to see here. Please go about your business. This was a misunderstanding that did not need to happen. I am not here to debate my father's politics or discuss the current situation with his campaign worker. I would appreciate it if everyone would leave me alone."

Doug quickly exited the store and the mall. As they got in the car, the agent asked him where he wanted to go next. Doug couldn't stop shaking; the encounter with the man, his hostility and words, upset Doug immeasurably. This was the first time anyone had ever directly attacked him over his dad's politics or actions; he was having trouble processing the incident.

The agent let Doug remain silent for a few moments; he had seen this before with other politicians' families he had guarded.

Doug finally let out a big sigh and said, "Let's just go back to the house. Hopefully this won't turn into another incident. I know you were just doing your job. Thank you." As they drove, Doug thought about all the cell phone cameras he had seen during the incident. *'This is going to show up all over the Internet before I even get home!'* His thoughts grew more morose.

Doug and the agent headed back to the house. When they arrived, the press was still there, camped out in front of the house. With the agent running interference, Doug pushed his way into the house without further incident.

Doug found his parents on the back porch, holding each other. His mom looked like she had been crying.

"Is everything all right between you two?" Doug asked with concern.

"We're fine, Doug. Your mother and I just needed to talk about all this. How was your trip to the mall?" Richard noticed his son looked upset.

"Well… " Doug began, looking down at his feet. "Not great. Someone recognized me at the mall and kind of made a scene in a store. He was shouting at me that you're a fraud and a liar who doesn't deserve anyone's vote anymore."

Doug paused to draw a deep breath before he went on, "He grabbed me by the arm when I tried to leave and my bodyguard put him on the ground. I apologized to him, but I don't know if he'll call the media or not. There was a pretty big crowd around us because of the scene he was making. Everyone seemed to have a camera phone. This is going to be all over the Internet, if it isn't already. Sorry Dad, I know this is the last thing you need to hear right now." Doug looked crestfallen.

Richard took all this in, moving over to put his arms around his son's shoulders.

"Doug, you couldn't have handled the situation any differently. I'm glad the agent was there to protect you. If that man or anyone else wants to make an issue out of this, so be it. These things come with the territory."

Doug looked up at his father gratefully. "Thanks Dad. I think I'll just keep a low profile until this is all over with."

Doug gave his father an embrace then headed up to his room. Richard and Donna watched him leave, then gave each other a concerned glance.

"It's already happening. Now this situation is directly affecting my family. I feel powerless to stop it!"

Donna reached out to embrace Richard. She murmured as she laid her head on his chest, "Don't worry Richard, we've raised smart and strong children. They'll handle themselves with the same dignity and respect they always have shown."

Doug went up to his room, sat down, and logged onto the

Internet. He Googled his own name, and there it was, already posted on someone's blog. As he read, his anger threatened to engulf him. *'How dare they!'* He raged inside. He stood up suddenly, walking over to look out into the night from his bedroom window, leaving the computer to sit there spewing its' hate. *'If I don't look, it can't hurt me. I wonder how Michelle is handling all this?'* She wasn't home. Doug remembered she was in class tonight.

At the moment Doug's thoughts were of his sister, she was in the bathroom of the University's science building, trying to calm herself down. She sat in the stall, her sides silently heaving, occasional small cries escaping despite her best efforts to block them.

'My own friends!' She was numb. She felt betrayed, cornered. She had only thought to escape, not attack; she had been caught so unaware.

'If this is what Dad's life is like, I don't know how he can stand it!' She thought. Her heart was still hammering, her temples pulsated with a roil of emotions that she could not singularly identify. *'This is too much. I can't live like this! How am I supposed to finish school after this?'* Her thoughts raced beyond her control.

Everything had been fine in class until her friend Laura had received a text message from someone; Michelle didn't know who. Laura had looked at Michelle, and then raised her hand. The professor had called on her and Laura had asked, "This is a political science class, right? Why don't we ask Miss Johnson how she can believe in her father's candidacy when he is so obviously a fraud?"

Michelle had been too stunned to even believe what she was hearing. She had known Laura for two years now. They were both studying to be nurses; she was the last person that Michelle believed would have attacked her publicly. Even more surprising was the animosity in her professor's voice as he replied, "Good question Laura. Miss Johnson, would you care to rebut?"

Normally not one to be slow on the uptake, Michelle could only stare silently as every head turned her way. Hot tears started to well up in her eyes.

"I, I, uh.." her voice failed her. She looked down at her desk, tears dripping, then began to gather her things to leave. She stood, excused herself down the row and walked up the stairs to the door. As she left, she could hear the laughter swell behind her. She had practically run down the hall to the bathroom.

Now, as she sat in the stall attempting to compose herself, she found that she was angry at her father. She had questions; he *had* to have some answers. She gathered her things, exited the stall, splashed some water on her face, then quietly left the restroom.

As she headed out to the parking lot to her car, her cell phone beeped. She pulled it out of her purse to see who had called; it was Laura sending her a text message. Without bothering to read it, Michelle closed her phone.

'Bitch!' Michelle was not normally someone who used a lot of curse words to express herself, but at this moment that word seemed to fit the situation. She found her car, unlocked the door, sitting for a moment before she got out her keys, started the car, and headed out of the parking lot and towards home.

When Michelle arrived home, she walked up the front steps and upon entering the house, threw her backpack down the entry hall. A minute later, she saw her mother then her father enter the hall and look her way. They could immediately see her distress.

"Michelle, what happened?" Donna rushed over to wrap her arms around her youngest child as Michelle burst into tears. The Secret Service agents walked in, hearing the commotion. Michelle had insisted that she be allowed to go to school unescorted; that would only bring more attention to the situation, she had argued. In the end, Richard had relented to his willful daughter.

"Daddy!" Michelle's wail took Richard back to a time when Michelle had been three years old. She had fallen off a box she had been playing on and skinned her knee. Richard, who had seen the whole thing, had rushed over, and hugged Michelle until she stopped crying. As he held her, he motioned to the agents that everything was alright and they left the room silently.

As she cried, he was hard-pressed to remember that she was a young woman now, not a child. *'They're always your children, no matter how old they get.'* He thought.

Richard walked up to Michelle and Donna and wrapped his arms around both of them. Doug had heard his sister's cry and came rushing downstairs to see his mother and father hugging his crying baby sister.

"Michelle, who did this!" Doug stood there, fists clenched, ready to fight the very air if necessary.

At the sight of Doug all puffed up like a peacock, Michelle couldn't help but giggle a little through her tears.

"Doug.." Michelle started to try and explain, but was overwhelmed by more tears. She thought with a chuckle, *'Is he the same brother that used to throw rocks at me? Now he's ready to save me!'* It was all too much. Richard, Donna, and Doug led Michelle into the living room, where they all sat down on the big couch, Michelle between Donna and Doug, with Richard pulling an ottoman over to sit facing his daughter.

Michelle finally composed herself enough to explain.

"I was in class, you know, tonight is my poli-sci class. Anyway, my friend Laura was looking at her phone under her desk and I think she got a text message that said something bad about you Dad." Michelle looked at her father with pleading eyes as she continued.

"Laura looked at me funny, then raised her hand and asked Professor Timmons to have me explain to the class why you were a fraud. I couldn't answer, Dad! I couldn't fight back! I just sat there; I was too shocked. I mean, Laura has been my friend for a long time!"

Richard and Donna glanced at each other. Doug added, in a quiet voice, "When I was up in my room just now, I was on the Internet. My squabble with that man is already all over the place.

That was probably where Laura's text message came from; one of her friends must have seen some of that stuff and sent her a message. I'm sorry, sis. I lost my temper." Doug cast his eyes downward.

Michelle took a deep breath, taking in all this new information. She glanced at Doug and spoke, "I guess we're all targets, now, huh? Don't worry about it, *big* brother. We'll handle this. Okay?" Her emphasis on the fact that Doug was older was not lost on him.

Doug looked into his sisters' eyes and found that she was looking at him with a clear, calm repose. He nodded gratefully.

Richard took his daughters' hands in his. He knew he needed to find a way to reassure both of his children that he was not at fault here. There *was* a logical explanation; he just didn't know what it was. Yet.

"Michelle, Doug." Richard began to address both of his children, his voice quiet yet full of conviction.

"I have *not*; repeat not, *ever* had an affair with anyone. This is going to get harder the longer Caroline stays in her coma. She is the only one who knows the truth. So far, we've been lucky as a family not to have to endure any personal attacks, except at me. That's part of being part of a politician's family. I cannot make everybody happy all the time. There *will* be people who attack us, sometimes for what seems to be no reason."

Doug cut in, "But Dad, this is personal! How can you stand these attacks?"

Richard smiled calmly at his still upset son. "Doug, you're a graduate student. You've been studying this field in detail for the past six years. Is this all so hard to understand? You know that this is what happens to politicians. We are under attack all the time. What can I say to reassure you that this is temporary?"

Doug glanced over at his sister, mother, then turned his gaze towards his father.

"Dad, I believe in you. I believe that did *not* have an affair. But.." Doug's voice trailed off. Doug looked at his father, almost sheepishly.

"How can *I* help you? I'm your son, not your campaign manager."

Richard chuckled as he replied, "Well, a good start would be not to get into anymore situations that end up on the Internet."

Michelle broke in, "How are we supposed to live our lives if people are going to attack us every where we go?"

At this, Donna spoke up. "Kids, you can help your father by supporting him. I've found out over the years that support takes many forms. Doug, you can help by controlling your temper. Michelle, you can help by not letting what happened tonight dictate your emotions."

Donna looked each of her children in the eyes. "Do you two understand what I'm saying?"

Doug and Michelle glanced at each other then looked at both their mother and father.

"We do," they responded in chorus.

Michelle spoke. "We've got your back, Dad! Don't we, Doug?"

Doug replied with enthusiasm, "It'll take a lot more than this to bring this family down!"

At that moment, Richard could not have been more proud of his family. *'We will make it through this in one piece! Even if I am not the President, I will always appreciate what Donna and I have built with this family!'* Richard's thoughts were only of his family at that moment.

Chapter 10

Investigation

Without Richard or anyone from his family or campaign talking to the press, Michael Wilson was hard-pressed for a story. He had seen the Internet picks and movies about Doug's confrontation in the mall, but he needed more. With Caroline in a coma, his girlfriend, the nurse attending her, wasn't getting any information for him, either. The guard posted at her door had not budged when Michael tried to get in to see Caroline. He decided to see if he could find out more about Caroline Hoffman.

He found out where she lived, and with camera and notebook in hand, went to her apartment building. He first tried the door, but it was locked. He then went to the apartment manager and managed to convince him that he was an associate of Caroline's who needed to get some paperwork from her apartment.

The manager seemed hesitant, but agreed to let him into her apartment. He hung around the doorway for a few minutes, but Michael told him that he had no idea where the paperwork was, and he would probably be awhile looking for it, but he promised to lock up before he left. At that, the manager went back to his office.

Michael turned and looked around the apartment. It was a small studio apartment, but very neat. There was a small kitchenette in one corner, and a door to the bathroom off of that. There were two large pictures hanging on one wall. One was of Richard Johnson, and the other was of a woman he did not recognize. He took a photo of the two pictures together. Directly under the pictures was a white iron daybed with a mauve colored comforter and what must have been a dozen pillows. The rest of the furnishings were white as well, which brightened the small room and made it seem more spacious. There was a coffee table and end table with a lamp on it, an armoire, and a 'baker's rack' with a small television, VCR/DVD player, and stereo on it. Over by the door was a white desk with a computer. He figured that would be the best place to begin looking.

He opened the drawers, looking for information. Inside of one of the drawers he found a large bag full of newspaper clippings about Richard Johnson. On one of the articles someone had written "This is your father" in felt pen above the picture of Richard. He took a photo of that. In another drawer he found some old photos dating back about 20 years. They looked to be family photos, one of a little girl sitting between a man that looked a lot like Richard and the woman from the picture on the wall. Another photo was dated about 24 years ago, and it was of a man that looked just like Richard Johnson had looked when he was younger. He took these two photos and put them in his jacket pocket. The other two drawers didn't contain much-- stationery, stamps, and a dictionary.

He looked in the armoire--nothing but clothes there. The kitchenette had a small table with two chairs, a mini-fridge, a microwave, and a sink. There were only kitchen items in those drawers. The bathroom was extremely small, nothing in the medicine cabinet but the usual items. There was a tiny closet in the bathroom, which held some towels on a shelf and some cleaning supplies.

'Oh well', Michael thought to himself, *'I should be able to use the pictures for something.'*

He locked the door on his way out, and stopped by the manager's office to thank him and left.

The next day the Seattle Times-Sentinel had both photos and the hand-written "This is your father," photo with an article entitled "Who Is This Mystery Girl? The article asked: Is she Richard Johnson's daughter or a person trying to slander his good name? Who is the woman sitting next to Richard Johnson in this old photo? Is this little girl Caroline Hoffman? Is she Richard Johnson's daughter?"

That morning, when Richard brought in the morning paper, he was shocked. He could not believe what he was seeing on the front page. *'How can this be? They must have superimposed his image over someone else's picture.'* He reluctantly took it into the kitchen to show Donna. She was going to see it anyway; might as well get it over with. He just set it on the counter in front of her.

"Oh no, Richard, how can this be happening? This is the Seattle Times-Sentinel, not the National Enquirer!" Donna started to cry. "Between this and all the Internet coverage Doug's altercation has gotten... I'm scared, Richard!" Richard walked around the counter and gathered her into his arms. He did not know what to say. He stood and stroked her hair for a while, then held her away from him so he could look her in the eyes. If he could have reached out and choked the life out of Michael Wilson at that moment, he would have.

"That is not a photograph of me. I have never seen either of those people in my entire life. Someone does not want me to be President, and we have to consider the fact that someone may have put Caroline up to this. I have to talk to Sue. You stay here, and do *not* answer the phone. Keep your cell phone on, though; I'll call you on it if I need to reach you, and you can call me on mine. I'm sure the phones at the campaign office are ringing off the hook." Richard left her in the kitchen to go and get dressed, then headed out. As he drove away, he could see the Secret Service agents following closely behind. *'This is going to be hard to get used to.'* he thought.

Richard went straight to the campaign office and marched into Sue's office.

Sue looked up, startled by his entrance. "Richard, this is getting worse, what are we going to do?"

"I know it is Sue, but I don't know what we can do. Did you look into DNA testing? Have you checked on Caroline's condition? Maybe she is awake today. No, they would have called me." Richard was talking to himself, as much as to Sue.

"The DNA testing does not give instantaneous results, neither does your blood types matching prove anything, so I suggest you go to the hospital just as soon as you can to begin. You can check on Caroline's condition at the same time. I will call the Seattle Times-Sentinel, and try to find out exactly who gave them these pictures and try to get a retraction. The man in this picture is not you, you're sure?" asked Sue.

"Absolutely. He looks a lot like me when I was younger, but I have never seen that woman in my life, so it is either of someone else or it is a fake," replied Richard.

"Richard, I have a friend in Portland, Arthur Raines, who used to be an investigative reporter for the Los Angeles Times. He retired a few years ago to Oregon due to his health, but he still takes jobs every now and then when I ask. I called him and asked him to look into Caroline's parents' backgrounds and let me know what he finds. As a personal favor to me, he has agreed to do it. I have already faxed him a copy of the article in this morning's paper. Now you had better get to the hospital so they can get started on the DNA testing." Richard headed to the hospital to do the DNA test. With that, Sue was already dialing the number for the Seattle Times-Sentinel, then, called Arthur Raines and explained the situation to him.

Arthur Raines drove to Stanford from Portland. He started very early the morning after Sue's call and arrived a little after 10 o'clock. While he was driving, he was thinking of where he was going to start. He decided to start at the local public library so that he could check the local newspapers about Caroline Hoffman. At the library, an older lady about 65 years old was at the counter.

Arthur asked her about seeing back issues of the local paper, and she said, "Sure, I can do that for you, just let me know the date you need."

He said, "How about 24 years ago?" and she replied, "You've got to be kidding!"

"No," he said, "I'm serious. I need some information about a family that lived here 25 years ago." Arthur turned on the charm that had served him so well all these past years.

"We don't save papers for that long, they're put on microfiche after ten years" she said, but went on helpfully, "I was born in this town, and I've lived here for more than 65 years; maybe I can help you." Raines was glad for an opportunity to get the information without scanning decades of microfiche newspapers.

"I am trying to get some information on the Hoffman family," said Arthur.

"You want to know about the Mystery Girl, right?" she asked, laughing. "I have had many reporters calling lately asking about her, but you're the first one to come in person. What would you like to know?"

"Did you know the Hoffman family?"

"Not well, Mrs. Hoffman used to come in once in a while to read the Seattle Times-Sentinel."

"How often did she come in?"

"I didn't keep track, I really couldn't tell you."

"Did she always come alone?"

"No, sometimes she had her little girl with her."

"She never came in with anyone else?"

"No, just alone, or with the girl. She would use the copy machine sometimes, photocopying some of the articles, and the little girl would want to push the button. I remember that. Kids are funny when a little thing like pushing the button is such a big deal to them."

Arthur pulled the fax out of his pocket, with the picture from the Seattle Times-Sentinel. "Is this Mrs. Hoffman in this picture?"

"Yes, it looks like how I remember her."

"Does she have any relatives here?"

"I think her father-in-law, Gary Hoffman, Sr., lives in a retirement home near the hospital."

"Can you tell me how to get to the hospital?"

"Why do you have so many questions about Mrs. Hoffman? I figured you were a reporter. Are you a cop or something?"

"No, I am just trying to get some information for a friend of mine. Never mind about the directions, I will find the hospital myself."

"It's okay, I'll tell you." Arthur's legendary charm was working perfectly. "I was just curious about all the questions. You take a left out of our parking lot, go to the light, and then take another left. It is the large building on your right, you can't miss it."

"Thanks, you have been a big help. Have a nice day now!" Arthur said, winking at her as he left the library.

Arthur decided to go to the retirement home to see if he could talk with Mr. Hoffman. When he arrived, he was shown to Mr. Hoffman's room. The older gentleman was lying in his bed, resting after lunch. He appeared surprised but pleased to have a visitor. Arthur said, "Mr. Hoffman, my name is Arthur Raines, and I would like to talk to you about your son."

"Oh, he died a long time ago. He was my only son," replied the old man.

"Was he your natural born son, or did you adopt him?"

"He was my son. After he was born, his mother and I couldn't have any more children. Gary died about 18 years ago."

"I'm sorry, how did he die?"

"He was sick with cancer."

"Do you remember who his doctor was?"

"Not his cancer doctor, but his regular doctor was Dr. Miles. He came to the funeral. He is a good man, that doctor. Why do you need to know who his doctor was?"

Arthur was not sure if he knew of Caroline's accident, and he did not want to upset the old guy. He decided it was better not to bring up Caroline Hoffman. She may or may not be his granddaughter.

"It is very complicated, and someone will explain it to you

later. Thank you so much for your help today, Mr. Hoffman," Arthur said, and left.

Arthur asked at the reception desk, "Can you tell me how to find Dr. Miles' office?"

He was told that Dr. Miles was semi-retired and was only in his office two days per week. The receptionist gave him directions to the office, and luck was with him that day because when he asked at the clinic, he was told that Dr. Miles was working that day. He had a full schedule, but if he could wait a few minutes, he could maybe speak with him in between patients. When he asked Dr. Miles about Gary Hoffman, he said he did not remember him. Arthur explained that he had died 18 years ago of cancer, and asked if he might see his files, but Dr. Miles explained that without permission from his next of kin, he could not allow him to see the file.

Arthur explained that he had just been speaking with Gary's father, and he had been the one that told him about Gary's cancer, and that Dr. Miles was his doctor. Dr. Miles offered to have his nurse bring the file up from the basement storage room if Arthur cared to wait until he had another moment in between patients to sit down with him. Arthur willingly agreed and settled down with a magazine in the waiting room. About 20 minutes later, the nurse called him over and showed him into Dr. Miles' office.

"What was it you needed to know?" asked the doctor.

Sue had told Arthur that Caroline had a rare blood type, and he had jotted it down in his notes. He asked Dr. Miles if this was the same blood type that Gary had had. He told him that there was a Caroline Hoffman lying unconscious in a hospital in Seattle, and we thought that Gary Hoffman had been her father. Dr. Miles looked through the file for a minute or two, and then looked up at Arthur.

"Mr. Raines, I am afraid you have the wrong guy. This patient not only had the wrong blood type, which wouldn't be conclusive anyway, but he was sterile, an unfortunate effect of his cancer treatment. This man could not be that girl's father." said Dr.

Miles.

'Well, that's that.' Thought Arthur ruefully. *'I got the information I came for. Too bad it isn't the information Sue wanted me to get. The girl really might be Richard Johnson's daughter.'*

When he got back into the car, he phoned Sue. He hated to give her the bad news, but she needed to know. When she answered the phone, he asked her, "Are you sure you want to hear this?"

"Bad news, huh? Go ahead, let me have it," Sue replied.

"Gary Hoffman is not Caroline's father. His blood type was wrong, but besides that, he was sterile. I know you were hoping I would confirm just the opposite, but there you go."

"Thanks Arthur, just send me your bill, and please keep this information to yourself."

"You bet, it will remain completely confidential. I hope you'll think of me again, if you ever need any more detective work done. I enjoyed getting back to work again, even if it was just for one day! Keep in touch, Sue!"

"You too, take care Arthur, and thanks." Sue hung up the phone, unsure of how to proceed.

Sue was about to call Richard and give him this information, but decided to wait a bit. The fewer people that knew, the better off they would be. She decided to wait and see what the DNA results were.

Tom Gibson had not been idle during this time. His phone call late in the night a few days ago had been a revelation. He decided to let Michael Wilson continue his investigation; Michael was right, Gibson did owe him big-time for this information. He had ordered Michael to track Sue Jacob, Richard's Campaign Manager. Michael had followed Arthur Raines as he made the rounds of the people he spoke with, so Gibson was well aware of what Raines had found out. Michael may be an ass, but he was a good reporter.

'Good things come to those who wait', he thought as he sat at

his desk. He now had a deal on the table to consider, and consider it carefully he would. Richard Johnson is going to lose now, and that felt good. Newman's campaign was continuing to press the trust issue with the public, and Gibson was well aware of where Richard's latest primary poll percentages were. Tom Gibson is now a hundred odd delegates above Richard and Richard was rapidly losing the support of both the public and his donor base. *'Yes, this is exactly where I need to be,'* he exulted to himself. *'Patience, patience, patience!'*

Chapter 11

The Connection

After Arthur's news, Sue sat back in her office and began to think back to when Caroline came to help with the election campaign. It was about a year ago when the news first broke about Richard Johnson's plans for candidacy. Richard was secretly working on fundraising with Sue to see if he could get enough support to even run. They had tried to keep his campaign a secret, but in this age of technology, that had proven to be problematic. It had been Michael Wilson and Gibson who had somehow found out about Richard's ambitions and broken the news to the press.

Richard did not like to take an unnecessary risk on anything. He always did his homework before he attempted to do anything. He had done the same thing when he decided to run for governor. He was a District Attorney at the time, and his wife Donna encouraged him to run for the position of Governor. Richard traveled to many small cities and towns all over Washington State to find out how much support he would receive if he did run for governor. When he was happy with the response, he decided to run.

He had done the same thing when considering running for President. He went all over the country see how much support he would receive. Political and business leaders all over the United States liked his style of management. Richard liked to get face to face with people to hear their opinions.

Richard was the first one to implement the idea that the

insurance companies should get involved in educating people on safety, health, and crime prevention so that the insurance rates would go down as a result of decreasing numbers of accidents and crimes. This had proven to be a win-win situation for insurance companies and the public alike. Quinn Flannery, funded heavily by the insurance companies, had opposed Richard's legislation and lost.

Sue mused to herself that today, the state of Washington was a much safer place to live and raise a family and insurance premiums were much lower than they were when he first took office in Olympia. This had been Richard's first big achievement in office and it had been a bitter fight, but in the end, he had won. His policies were adopted by several other states. Politicians and business leaders around the country found that his style and approach were good for both businesses and the people.

About a year ago, when Richard was considering running for President, his picture was all over the newspapers, and people began speculating on whether or not Richard would actually run. At that time, Sue recalled, was when she received a call from a young girl named Caroline Hoffman.

Caroline had said, "I've been hearing that Richard Johnson may be running for the Presidency, and I would like be a volunteer on his campaign staff."

Sue had told her that Richard had not yet made up his mind. She offered to send Caroline an application, and as soon as he had made his decision, she would give Caroline a call. Caroline agreed to this and gave Sue her address.

The next week, Sue received a package from Caroline with her background information and an explanation of why she considered Richard Johnson to be a good candidate for the Presidency, and why she wanted to help him get elected.

'Now that I think about it, Caroline had written that Richard reminded her of her father, and she said she would like to help get a man like her father elected as President of the United States.

Funny I did not remember this before now!' Sue thought to herself.

Caroline had called every other week asking if he had made up his mind yet. About six months later, Richard made his decision, partly driven by the press generated by Michael Wilson.

Sue did not have to call Caroline; *she* had called that same day asking, "Has he made up his mind?"

"Yes, Caroline, he has decided to run. We can use your help. Please, come up to Seattle and join our campaign," Sue had said.

Within two days Caroline was there, and Sue was impressed with her prompt arrival. Sue had introduced her to Richard, and she seemed so excited to meet him. That was all she could remember about Caroline's joining their team.

Sue sat, lost in her recollections. *'Just who was Caroline Hoffman, really? Why had she been so eager to help Richard? What is her connection to Richard? There definitely was a connection. She just needs to come out of this coma, and tell us what it is!'*

Chapter 12

Leeches

Doug decided it was time to pay Caroline a visit. He still doubted she wanted to see him, but she was not waking up. Maybe if he went to the hospital and apologized, she would hear him, and maybe then she would wake up. It was worth a try. As he drove to the hospital, he thought back over the time since he had met Caroline.

They had gone out quite a few times, but never alone; never just the two of them. They had gone to a Mariner's game with Kevin and Beth, which had been a lot of fun. They had gone to the zoo with Jeremy and Beth, but Caroline seemed to pay more attention to Jeremy than to him. They had spent the day on the waterfront once, and gone on a harbor tour during sunset. Beth and Kevin and Jeremy and Michelle had all come along that day. During the tour, Doug had tried to get Caroline alone at the front of the boat. The sunset was so romantic and all, but she would always call one of the others over. She had always been nice to him, but friendly-nice, nothing more. Whenever he had tried to hold her hand or put his arm around her, she would pull her hand back, or move out of his arm. Not in a mean way, just smoothly moving out of the contact. She treated him more like a 'buddy' or a brother. That was *not* what Doug wanted, though; he wanted her to like him like she would a boyfriend.

He had even wondered if she was a lesbian at one point. He

had made it clear to her that he was interested in her. She *had* to know. She never talked about a boyfriend, so it wasn't that. Whenever he and his father had quarreled, she would take his father's side. Once when they were all having dinner together, he had asked his dad if he could buy a new car. His dad had agreed that it was time he had a car of his own, and Doug told him he wanted a Porsche 911. His dad had explained that he could have a new car, but certainly not an expensive sports car.

"A car is a means of transportation to get you from one place to another." Richard had explained. "It is not a status symbol, to show off or drive fast. I'll buy you a sensible, safe vehicle, Doug."

Caroline had agreed with Richard and said, "There are several issues here, Doug. If people see you driving around in a Porsche, people will think that the Governor makes way too much money if he's able to afford a car like that for his son. Also, sports cars aren't safe. Since they are powerful cars, you know you'd be tempted to drive fast and see what it can really do, and that's dangerous. Your dad is worried about your safety. Besides, do you know how much it would cost to insure you to drive one of those things?"

Doug could remember thinking, *'Who does she think she is, butting into a family matter like this? It isn't any of her business what kind of car I drive, anyway.'*

Doug could not help but think...

'Maybe she really does think of herself as part of our family. She said she was my sister. She said my dad was her dad. She is somehow immune to my charms (ha ha). She came all the way from California to help with his campaign. She and I are about the same age, and my dad was in the town where she was born, in the year before she was born. Could my dad really have had an affair? I hate to think about it, but what other explanation could there be?'

He pulled in to the parking garage and, shoving all these thoughts aside, pushed his way through the reporters. He headed to the gift shop first to get some flowers for Caroline.

He could see all the newspaper and magazines laid out in the gift shop. He looked in disgust as a local newspaper in Stanford was reporting that a woman was claiming to have had an affair with Richard Johnson, and that Caroline was her daughter; a result of that affair. She had claimed she had given her up. She claimed the Hoffman's had adopted her. Her name was Camille Church, and she was about 40 years old. Investigative reporters soon found out she was a fraud. She had made the whole story up, to get her "15 minutes of fame", as Andy Warhol had famously stated, and probably to try to swindle some money out of Richard Johnson. She had been arrested and charged with malicious slander, but Richard had declined to press charges.

A librarian from a public library in Palo Alto had been interviewed and informed the newspapers that she had known Caroline's real mother, a woman named Irene Hoffman. She went on to say she had observed Irene visiting the library often over a ten year period, and she had frequently seen her reading and photocopying articles about Richard Johnson. Doug knew from Arthur Raines' report to Sue that the librarian was a nice lady; she probably thought her comments to be innocent. *'The media will use anyone to get to my dad',* Doug thought.

As the librarian's comments became more widely known, support for Richard had continued its downward spiral. The latest delegate numbers are 40% compared to Tom Gibson. Sue Jacob had told Doug she was afraid to even watch the news, knowing it would only be more scandal, hurting their campaign efforts more with every newscast. Doug turned away from all the newspapers and magazines paid for the bouquet and headed up to see Caroline.

Doug had picked out a beautiful bouquet of peach colored roses when he ran into Beth in the hallway just down the hall from Caroline's room.

"Hi Doug! Those roses are gorgeous, Caroline will love them!"

"Hi Beth. Were you in Caroline's room, is she awake yet?"

"No, I was just on my way to see her. You go ahead, I can wait."

"Why don't you go ahead of me, I'm still not sure what I'm going to say. I need a few minutes to think, anyway."

"Okay, I won't be long. This is the first time I've been here since the accident, so I'm anxious to see how she is doing."

Beth continued down the hall and turned to go into Caroline's room, but the guard at the door stopped her and asked who she was. When she told him she was Caroline's friend Beth, he informed her that she was not on the list of who was allowed to visit, and she would not be allowed in. Doug heard what was being said, and hurried down the hall.

"I'm Doug Johnson, officer, the Governor's son. She's okay. She was with Caroline the night of the accident. She can go in," said Doug.

"I am sorry sir," said the guard, "I have orders not to allow anyone not on this list."

Doug called his mom from his cell phone and asked her for the police chief's phone number. He then called the chief.

"Tom, this is Doug Johnson. I'm at the hospital, outside Caroline's room, and I want to ask you a favor. Can you please add Beth's name to the visitor's list, so she can see Caroline? I can put your guard on the phone now."

The guard spoke to the chief, and then he added Beth's name to the list on his clipboard.

"Thank you officer, I really appreciate it. I am grateful you are so careful. The media is having a field day with this situation, the last thing we need is to have one of them sneak into Caroline's room." He then left Beth to her visit, and went to think about what he was going to say to Caroline when it was his turn.

Beth only stayed a few minutes and walked over to Doug when she was through.

"Your turn Doug," she said. "She's still unconscious, but she just looks like she's sleeping."

Doug picked up his flowers and headed down to Caroline's room. He walked in and set them next to her bed. She was lying there so peacefully. There were not nearly as many tubes, wires, and devices connected to her as there had been the night of the accident. One tube was obviously an IV, in her left arm; there was an automatic blood pressure cuff wrapped around her upper right arm. The wires were monitoring her heartbeat. She had been cleaned up this time, with just a smallish bandage on her head. She had a few scrapes and bruises around her mouth and nose. Doug didn't have much experience seeing people in this condition; the antiseptic smell, the beeping of the machines all added to his already nervous state of mind. He pulled a chair up next to her bed, and took her hand.

A long moment passed before Doug spoke, "Caroline, I am *so* sorry. I feel like this is all my fault. The whole time that I have known you, you have never led me to believe that you were interested in me as more than a friend. I just felt like there was something between us, some kind of connection. I just thought if you would give it a chance, you would feel it too. I thought that if I kissed you, maybe you would see that there could be something there. I had no right to do that. I don't blame you for running out of the club that night."

Doug tried to compose himself; hot tears were welling in his eyes. His voice trembled with emotion as he went on, "I'm really confused about this whole 'sister' thing though."

Doug tried to look at her face as he spoke. "What did you mean by that? Why did you tell that doctor that my dad was your dad? This is really damaging him in the polls, and you've worked so hard on his campaign! It just doesn't make any sense. I wish you would wake up, so you could clear all of this up!"

Doug had regained his composure as soon as he had poured out his emotions. He didn't really want to say what he said next; he still wanted to hope that he and Caroline could be a couple. But he was his father's son; whose values had been instilled in Doug from a young age.

"I respect your decision to just be friends. I won't try anything again, and I would like to remain friends if you'll still have me. Just please get well, and talk to us again."

Doug sat there for quite awhile in silence, then stood up, and started to lean over to kiss her on the forehead, but thought better of it. He put the chair back and slowly walked out of the room. He walked back up the hall, and to his surprise, Beth was still sitting there.

"How did it go Doug, do you feel any better?" Beth asked.

"Yeah, a little, I guess. I needed to apologize and let her know I was okay with just being friends. I heard somewhere that comatose patients can hear things around them. Maybe she heard me. I just wish she would wake up."

"I am sure she heard you, and she will wake up soon. Why don't you let me buy you a latte? I saw an espresso stand on the first floor." Beth put a hand on Doug's shoulder and walked him to the elevator.

Michael Wilson moved from his spot around the corner from Caroline's room. The guard had not budged this time, either, when he had attempted to get inside claiming to be one of Caroline's friends, so he had employed some technology. A small microphone, designed to pick up noise from 1,000 yards away, was in his hands, plugged into a digital recorder. He had picked up the whole conversation. He had what he needed for now, since his nurse girlfriend had dried up as a source. This was a whole new angle to the situation: The Candidate's son was in love with Caroline! He rushed out, keeping a low profile, and headed off to his office at the Times-Sentinel.

On the way to his office, Wilson got on his cell phone and called Tom Gibson to tell him what he had found out. He asked Gibson what he was going to do with this new information; he was a little dismayed at Gibson's answer: he seemed distant and uninterested.

'Just what is going on here?' Michael asked himself as he hung up. *'Gibson should be eating this up! This could be the last nail in Johnson's political coffin, but Gibson doesn't seem to care. Why?'* Michael decided that it didn't matter what Gibson did or

didn't do with his info; he was still going to break this news. *'Maybe Newman would be interested in this story angle. I know he's looking for more to use against Johnson.'*

Upon arriving at his office Michael sat down and began to type.

Tom Gibson was lost in his own thoughts. Wilson's phone call with this new angle to the rapidly expanding scandal with Johnson *should* have excited him, but for some reason, it did not. For the first time since all this happened, he felt himself at a crossroads. He had been giving serious thought to Richard's proposal and had, for the time being, honored Richard's request.

This felt different, though. *'This is getting too personal. This is Richard's son! I have a son, how would I feel about his being sucked into something I created? Would I be willing to preserve my political career by throwing my son to the wolves?'* Gibson thoughts were now of his own family and how they had dealt with his political career. They had stood by him steadfastly; not unlike Richard's family. He would have to carefully think about his response to this information.

Chapter 13

Surprise

The next morning, Richard was awakened to a ringing phone. Sue Jacob told him to meet her at the hospital right away. The results from the DNA testing were in. As soon as they were revealed, she wanted to schedule a press conference. He agreed to meet her there in one hour.

When Richard arrived at the hospital, Sue was right there to meet him. She walked him to the elevator, talking the whole way. "Have you seen the polls Richard? It's really bad! That woman in California was a fraud, but the public doesn't seem to care. You did the right thing in not pressing charges against her, though. It makes you look fair and compassionate. We need all the positive press we can get right now."

Sue went on breathlessly, "Do you think the librarian is lying too? Why would Irene Hoffman, if she exists at all, follow your career all these years? Arthur didn't give me the impression that she was anything but nice; but I guess you never know. I only hope now that we have the DNA test as proof, we can correct the damage that has been done. The doctor wants to see you alone to give you the results. I will wait here. He said he would meet you down this hall, fourth door on the left."

Richard had not been able to get one word in the whole conversation. '*Sue is certainly worked up this morning. These test results should calm her down,*' thought Richard. He knocked on the door, and was answered with an invitation to enter. He walked in, and the doctor walked over and shook his hand.

"Good morning Governor, I am Dr. Swanson. Please, have a seat," offered the doctor. "I am afraid these are not the results you were probably hoping for. The test shows that your DNA matches Caroline Hoffman's. I'm sorry, sir."

Richard was flabbergasted. "That is impossible doctor! What are the chances that an error occurred in testing? I have never been with anyone, other than my wife. I *know* she isn't my daughter. What other explanation could there be?"

"Well, she *could* be your father's child," answered the doctor, trying to he helpful. "Other than that, I don't know what to tell you. We used the latest technology for your test. These tests are very accurate, and because of your standing in the community and the current situation, we double-checked the results. The results are very clear: Caroline *is* related to you."

Richard walked out of the doctor's office in shock. He had truly expected to be told that the results proved that it was impossible for Caroline to be his daughter. This was unbelievable. *'Could his dad have had an affair and Caroline be his sister?'* It was preposterous to even think of it. He walked over to Sue, and she knew before he even said a word. Her stomach felt like it had dropped to the floor.

'Oh no,' Sue thought, *'it was true. Richard had had an affair. He had been lying about Caroline being his daughter. This was it. The campaign was finished.'* She walked over and put her hand on Richard's arm. "Richard, what were the results, does it prove she isn't your daughter?" she asked.

"No Sue, just the opposite; the test was positive. I am related to Caroline. The doctor was adamant about the accuracy of the test. The only other possibility is that she could be my dad's daughter, not mine. That would make her my sister. Can you see my dad having an affair?"

"That's it! That has to be the answer! Oh Richard, that is wonderful news! I never even thought of that possibility. Are you going to call him? You know you need to; it might save your campaign!" Sue was so relieved.

"Sue, listen to what you are saying. I do not believe my father had an affair twenty five years ago. He would have been around 50 years old." *'I'm almost 50,'* thought Richard, and all of a sudden it did not seem that impossible. "I can't just call my dad and ask him if he had an affair with some woman years ago. That would just be too disrespectful."

"Richard, if you don't find out the truth, you can kiss the presidency goodbye. This is killing your political career; you have *got* to do *something*!" Sue pleaded.

"Sue, word of this is going to get out, and I think it is best we announce it to the press ourselves. I would like you to hold a press conference without me and make the announcement as soon as possible. I am going to go home and tell Donna and the kids before they hear it on the news. I need you to do one other thing for me. I need you to call Arthur Raines and see if he can get access to Irene Hoffman's medical records and check her blood type. He needs to see if she is either Type A or B, positive or negative." Sue agreed and Richard left Sue standing there, while he walked slowly down the hall to the elevator.

Later that afternoon, Sue held the press conference while Richard and his family watched it on TV from their home. Sue confirmed to the press that a DNA test had been conducted on both Richard and Caroline; the result being that Richard was somehow related to Caroline. She stressed that this did *not* prove that Caroline was Richard's daughter; just that they were related. She took no questions from the press.

None of them knew what to think when Richard told them. They chose to believe Richard, and they all wished there was some explanation to this whole mess. After Sue announced that Richard and Caroline's DNA belonged to the same family, Richard dropped another 10 points in the polls. The press began investigating Caroline's past, and that of her parents.

The news was filled with new bits of information, some of it inaccurate, every day. Caroline's mother *was* Irene Hoffman, and the man who had been thought to be her father was Greg Hoffman. Greg Hoffman was an accountant, and had died of leukemia 18 years ago. Caroline's mother had been a nurse, and had died of heart disease at the age of 50. Greg Hoffman's father was still alive, and had been interviewed by several reporters. Mr. Hoffman confirmed that Greg was his son, and they had no family connection to Richard. Greg had been his only son and Caroline was his only grandchild. Their family seemed to be an average family with no scandals to be found. Caroline had been a straight A student, and had not been in any trouble.

Richard and Donna watched every news report with interest. Who were the Hoffman's? Neither of them could remember having ever met, nor seen these people when they were living in Stanford. How could Caroline have Johnson DNA? The answers had to come from Caroline or Richard's father, but Caroline was still lying silently in the hospital, not knowing all that was going on about her and Richard was loathe to speak with his father about this issue, campaign or no campaign. Richard checked on her condition every couple of hours. Her body was functioning normally, but she had not regained consciousness. Sue had called a little while ago. Raines had been able to get hold of Irene Hoffman's medical records, which indicated that Irene was indeed blood Type A positive. What this meant, Richard didn't know. Richard had told Sue to expect him back at the office within the hour; he was going to hold his own press conference. Sue had told him that most of the media were still camped outside his office; she would let them know he was coming to speak in person. She cautioned him about giving too much information, though, since there were other possibilities about why their DNA matched. Richard agreed and, after giving Donna and his children a hug, left for the campaign office.

Richard walked into the main hall of his campaign headquarters without his usual smile.

He could see reporters everywhere. Microphones had been placed on his podium. The hall was quiet as Richard walked up to the podium to address the assembled media. Somberly, he began to speak.

"Good evening ladies and gentlemen. I will attempt to explain the medical information I have been given and it will then become your decision as to whether you believe me or not. Following my statement I'll answer a few of your questions. I only wish there was another explanation to offer you."

Richard paused, took a deep breath, and continued.

"I took a DNA test and the results came back today. It shows that Caroline Hoffman and I are from the same family."

The crowd began to murmur, noise swelling from the back of the hall to the front as Richard continued to speak.

"Yes, it's a great surprise for me, too. What I can swear to you is that I have *never* had any kind of relationship with anyone other than my wife. She was my high school sweetheart. I love her very much and she loves me very much. This news is hurting her and my children more than it's hurting my election. Today we live in a world of science and technology. Science has done a lot of great things for us, and now that same science is telling us that Caroline Hoffman belongs in my family. I don't know how, but it's a fact. Now, would you kindly show some thoughtful consideration before asking any questions."

Reporters instantly began raising their hands and shouting out questions. Richard pointed to a female reporter who'd been a supporter of his campaign in the past.

"Yes, Jacquelyn."

Jacquelyn Harris, known for her fair and accurate reporting, instead asked what everyone wanted to know, "Governor Johnson, how do you feel knowing that you have another daughter?"

Richard tried to calm himself as he answered.

"The test simply reveals that we are related. She could in fact be my sister or perhaps the daughter of a close family member. Nothing proves that she is my daughter."

At this, Michael Wilson jumped in without waiting for

Richard's acknowledgement, "Governor, we have three separate points of proof that implicate you as her father. First, the blood test; second, she told the doctors that you are her dad. And third, the DNA test. Why should people believe you?"

Richard glared at Wilson as he replied, "First, and most importantly, my wife and family believe me, because they *know* me. I've *never* had relations with anyone other than my wife. It's up to the people to believe me or not. I have always told the people the truth and I have faith that they will use their intelligence to judge this situation fairly. All we can do now is wait until Caroline Hoffman regains consciousness. Then, and only then, will we know the whole truth."

Richard pointed at another reporter, who asked, "What happens if Ms. Hoffman doesn't regain consciousness or ends up too brain-damaged to speak? What happens then?"

Richard replied with conviction in his voice, "I have faith in God, and I firmly believe that she will regain consciousness and tell the truth soon. That is all I have to say for now. Thank you all for coming." Richard then walked away from the podium to shouts of, "Governor, Governor please!" from the reporters.

Chapter 14

Eroding Support

Richard went to his office, his two Secret Service agents placing themselves outside his door. He gave them instructions that no one except for Sue Jacob or a member of his immediate family was to be admitted. *'At least they'll keep everyone out of here so I can think,'* Richard thought, grateful for the first time for their presence. Almost before he sat down, the cell phone rang.

Richard sighed, picking up, "Hello, this is Richard Johnson." On the other end was one of his long-time Democratic supporters, Joyce Richmond. Joyce had been elected to the State of Washington's House of Representatives a year after Richard had been elected Governor, and like Richard, was a moderate Democrat. They had worked together on many different projects and Richard had always been able to count on her support. She had, in fact, been one of the strongest supporters of his decision to make a bid for the Presidency.

"Hello Richard, this is Joyce. How are you holding up?"

"As well as I can under the circumstances. I suppose you just caught the press conference?"

"Yes, I did. Richard, you know I have *always* believed in both you as a person and as a politician, but this..." Joyce let her voice trail off. "I don't quite know how to say this to you, but this scandal is embarrassing the Party. I'm sure I don't have to tell you that Tom Gibson and Newman are using this for all it's worth. We're *all* paying a price here, Richard, not just you."

Richard sat back, stunned at the implications of Joyce's words. He didn't know if he was up to hearing what she seemed about to say.

"Richard, I've been having some conversations with other Party supporters of yours. The news is not positive for you, you have to know that."

"Joyce, are you telling me that I'm going to lose your support?"

Joyce was silent for a moment, as if carefully considering her reply. If she withdrew her support, others would follow like lemmings over a cliff. She finally spoke.

"This situation *has* to be resolved now, Richard. I just got off the phone with Don Hallowell." Hallowell was a well-respected and powerful Democratic Senator from California who was a strong supporter of Richard's bid for President. He had publicly stated more than once that he had never known a more trustworthy person. If Richard lost him *and* Joyce, his bid was over.

Joyce continued, "He's leaving his decision whether to withdraw support up to me. Just between you and I, though, he's ready to jump ship and back Tom Gibson. What assurances can you give me that you're telling us the truth? The evidence seems pretty strong that you're the girl's father. We do *not* need a repeat of the Clinton mess."

Richard tried to muster up any emotion that wasn't anger. *'How dare they question him now, of all times!'* His stomach churned as he answered Joyce's question.

"Joyce, I have dedicated my life to being a man of principle, of honesty, and I have tried to do the best I could for the people of Washington and still maintain these values. I would stake the lives of my children when I say to you that, *I have not ever had an affair with anyone!*"

Richard was practically shouting now, and had to take a deep calming breath before he continued.

"Joyce, I need you and Don now more than ever to think back to any time I have ever let you both or the people down as far as

109

my ethics and honesty are concerned and have some faith that this is *not* what it seems. There is an explanation that makes sense somewhere out there and if you will give me some more time, I promise you it will turn out not to be the scandal that people want it to be." Richards' hands were shaking as he finished.

Joyce replied quickly, "Richard, you know that Don and I believe in you. If we didn't, we wouldn't be having this conversation privately; you'd be hearing about it in the press. We can't give you much more time before we *need* to make a decision. I will call Don and tell him I'm still on board with you, but only for now. You don't have much more time. Convention is around the corner and super delegates are watching the news and asking questions. I would suggest you give John Farrelly a call as well. He needs to hear from you the same thing you just told me."

Richard, thankful for small victories, replied, "Thank you Joyce. I won't let you down. And you're right about John; I'll call him tonight. Thank you."

"Don't make me regret this Richard. This is serious. But I believe you have earned the right to be proven wrong before you are crucified. I'll do what I can for now."

Joyce hung up and Richard immediately dialed John Farrelly's office. He hoped John was still there. John was a powerful elder-statesman type Democratic Senator from Idaho; his support was crucial as well for Richard's success.

He was able to get through to John on the first try. John had almost the same things to say as Joyce, albeit in a more paternal manner. John had been in office for decades, his advice was invaluable. Richard repeated what he had asked of Joyce. John's response was the same: Richard had earned the right to their support for now, but he did not have much time left to resolve this matter. Richard thanked him, hung up the phone, and sat back in his chair to think.

These were powerful people. *'And they believe in me still!'* Richard couldn't help but be amazed that these people, who held so much sway over both the people and fellow Democrat's opinions were willing to give him some more time.

'Caroline, dammit, you have to wake up soon!' With that thought echoing through his mind, Richard got up, turned off the office lights, and with his two agents trailing behind like ghosts, left for home.

Chapter 15

Family Decision

On his way home, Richard called Sue and asked her to come over for dinner, even though it was late. He needed his family, including Sue, to help him decide what to do about the campaign. He did not want to continue, unless he was sure he could win; however, he was no quitter either. He did not like the position he was in, and since it affected every one of them, he decided that a joint decision was in order. Richard recounted the conversations he had just had with Joyce Richmond and John Farrelly, as well as what Don Hallowell had said to Joyce. He let them all know that he had been successful in gaining a few more days before his campaign lost their support.

Sue informed them that Richard's popularity was at the bottom, the latest reports had him at 20% approval in the next three states going to have the primary. Tom Gibson is out there campaigning both day and night. Richard had lost most of their financial backing. With the final primaries and caucuses around the country being held soon, they needed to think about other ways of winning delegates. The super-delegates were crucial. Doug's encounter with the man in the mall was still big news on both the Internet and national news. Things were grim. Richard could tell that they were all hesitant to fully express themselves, so he told them, "Just say it! Anyone? I know you all have questions, so ask them. Now is the time."

Doug was the first to speak. "Dad, you know we all believe in you or we wouldn't be here. Yes, this has been hard on all of us. Your career is in jeopardy. But I'll say it again: we believe in you! You need to have the same belief in yourself that we have."

Heads nodded in agreement as Doug spoke. As Richard looked intently at each and every one of them, he couldn't help but feel overwhelmed by their unconditional love and support.

"You're right Doug. Thank you all for your support and your love for me. I promise this will all work out the way it is supposed to." Richard had to fight back tears as he spoke.

Sue spoke up. "Look, we don't have to win all the next primaries and caucuses; we just have to win more delegates, especially the super delegates."

Sue looked at everyone. "If we win enough delegates in the upcoming primaries and caucuses as well as the super delegates, it could force the nomination to be decided at the Convention. By then, hopefully, this will all be resolved."

Sue went on, "Doug, you know how this works, right?"

Doug nodded as he replied, "Dad, she's right. All we need to do is stay in the race. We don't have to win all the remaining primaries and caucuses. We just need to keep winning delegates. Maybe we could adjust the campaign a little and focus on that. Then, hopefully by the time the Democratic Convention roles around, Caroline will have awakened."

They all decided that since Richard believed he was innocent and knew there was a good explanation out there then they would stick it out. This meant too much to all of them. They had all worked too long and sacrificed too much to quit now. They were going to change the world, remember?

Before retiring that evening Richard decided to call his father. He was unsure of his decision but it was his last option. Donna walked over and gave him a kiss, "Ready to call it a day?" she asked.

"I think I am going to stay up for just a little longer, you go ahead. I'll use my downstairs study, so I won't disturb you." answered Richard.

"Okay, don't stay up too late. I know you are really stressed out, but there isn't anything more you can do about it tonight, you know. I love you!" Donna said.

Richard walked downstairs to the study and picked up the phone. He started to dial, but hung it up before it could connect. No one would ever want to call someone with a question like this anyway, but this was his dad for goodness sake! How do you ask your own father if he had an affair 25 years ago? Richard respected his father very much and knew the answer would be no, but he simply had to ask. He was up against a wall. He had never been with any woman other than Donna in his entire life.

However they shared the same blood type and even more damaging was that their DNA matched. Caroline was definitely related. Maybe his dad had gone to a sperm bank, or maybe he had fathered a child before he met mom that was given up for adoption. Those would be much easier questions than "Did you have an affair". Much better. Now he could make the call. He picked the phone up again, and this time he completed the call.

"Hello?"

"Dad, it's Richard."

"Hey son, I have been watching the news, I didn't have the strength to call you. I was waiting for your call... I haven't heard from you for a few days. How is that Caroline girl doing? Any answers yet?" *'Right to the point,'* Richard thought. His father was not one for small talk.

"No Dad, she is still unconscious. I haven't called because there has not been anything new to tell you, until now. I had a DNA test done, and it shows that Caroline's DNA and my DNA are from the same family. She is related to me somehow. I wouldn't be calling you with a question like this, but since I am an only child, it is either you or me. Dad, have you ever donated to a sperm bank, or did you have a serious relationship before you met mom? Maybe Caroline is my sister and not my daughter." There was silence on the other end of the phone. "Dad? Say something!"

His father finally answered, "I was just trying to think Richard.

I have had a long life, it takes awhile to remember my whole adult life, you know? There's a lot at stake for you here."

"Take your time, Dad, I'm sorry. I just thought you might get angry about my asking. I thought you might think I was trying to push my problem off on you. I just know that I have never been to a sperm bank, and I have never been with anyone but Donna, so I had to ask you."

"Of course I wouldn't get angry, son. And I know you didn't ask me, but no, I have never cheated on your mother. I did have one relationship before her, but I remained good friends with the girl for a few years after our relationship ended. And this was before you were born, so I am absolutely certain I would have known if she had a baby."

"What about donating to a sperm bank, ever done that?"

"No, never did. Sorry son, not much help, was I?"

"That's okay Dad. At least I'm not left wondering. The only one that can be of any help now is Caroline. I just wish she would regain consciousness."

"What are the doctors saying? How is she doing?"

"She is doing well, healing nicely, except for the fact that she won't wake up."

"Give it time Richard; the good Lord will take care of everything for you. With Him on your side, there is just no reason for this worry, you know. Let the kids know I'm thinking' about them."

"I know, thanks Dad, and I will. You really have been a help to me tonight. Tell you when I get to the White House, I'll have you over for dinner, okay?" Richard laughed.

His father chuckled as he replied back, "You bet son, I'll be taking you up on that offer before you know it! Remember what got you to where you are today, son. No one can take your accomplishments away. I trust that the truth will come out soon and you will win."

"I hope so. You have a nice night Dad, thanks for being so understanding. I love you."

"I love you too, son. Now get some sleep. Goodnight."

With that, Richard hung up the phone and headed up to bed. He would tell Donna about their conversation in the morning. At least he was not left wondering any longer, but it just made the situation even more mysterious. The jaded politician in Richard, which remained a side of himself he hated, still debated if his father had been truthful? With politics one never knew who could be absolutely trusted.

Chapter 16

The Real Politics

For the next couple days, support for Richard's campaign continued to erode. The media, the people, fellow Democrats; they all began to really believe that Richard was lying to them about Caroline. Her continued silence hurt him more with every passing day; what made it worse was there was absolutely nothing he could do to speed up her recovery. He had never felt so powerless in his life.

His financial backing had all but dried up; he had begun to let some of his junior campaign staffers go because he simply couldn't continue to pay them. Richard's campaign was running on fumes. Many of the campaigners were willing to forgo their salary and volunteer. They were willing to work for free because of the trust they had in Richard.

There were people who continued to believe that Richard was innocent until it was proven that he was guilty, but the media seemed not to want to report the opinions of those people; only that America's darling politician was plummeting from grace.

With the final primaries and caucuses only weeks away, Richard found himself wondering often if he would show up in the polling, let alone win the nomination. John, Joyce and Don, including many of his strongest supporters had gradually distanced themselves. They weren't coming right out and condemning him, but their comments about his main competitor for the nomination, Tom Gibson, told him all he needed to know.

Numerous polls had his support level so low that even Republican Vice-President Newman had stopped talking about Richard. *'You can beat a dead horse only so long before people stop watching,'* Richard thought as he caught one of Newman's many campaign speeches. *'He thinks I won't survive this at all.'*

Despite all of this, Richard had continued to give interviews to anyone who would have him, as well as continuing with his campaign itinerary. He and Sue had agreed that even with a skeleton campaign staff, to just hold up and ignore everyone was not acceptable. Everywhere he went, every time he spoke publicly, no one seemed to care about his policies, just his connection to Caroline Hoffman.

He stuck to his core message of family values, repeating them in speeches so often it felt to Richard like a mantra he was using to convince himself that he wasn't a fraud. Some people met him with a mixture of skepticism and at times outright hostility.

Almost all the media outlets and commentators gave Richard little to no chance of winning the nomination. There were even a few of his more vocal critics calling for him to withdraw from the race altogether. They all kept focusing on how he had betrayed the trust of the people, that he was a fraud; no matter his accomplishments as Governor of Washington.

Catching another interview with Gibson one night, Richard could only watch in disgust as Gibson danced around the subject of why he had not yet come right out to declare his candidacy now that Governor Johnson was disgraced. *'Serves me right for ever trusting that slug!'* Richard thought. *'How quickly people forget. Maybe it is true that nice guys finish last. Well, they haven't beaten me yet!'* The fighter within Richard just wouldn't allow him to give up, even now. He still had hope that Caroline would awaken soon and set things straight. *'Believe in yourself, that's what got you this far!'*

Chapter 17

The Mystery Girl Wakes Up

A week later, Richard awoke to a phone call in the middle of the night. The doctor told him that Caroline was getting better. Over the past few weeks, they had been gradually reducing the medication that was keeping her in the coma, to the point that she was now able to move a little, as well as beginning to speak. She should continue to improve every day, he was told. But she was confused and her memory was not clear as to what had happened. Richard was happy and relieved to hear this. He was not only happy to hear the news because the mystery might soon be solved, but he was genuinely happy that Caroline was out of danger and on the mend. He was trying to wait patiently for her to get well. The doctors were refusing to let anyone in to see her during this time, not even Richard or any member of his family. She was too fragile still.

The next few days were torture for the Johnson family. The doctors updated Richard often on her condition, though. She had not asked for him, but she had talked to the doctors and nurses a bit. Richard had found out a while back that Caroline's nurse in the beginning was the one who had called Michael Wilson and broken the story. Richard had demanded that she be replaced. The hospital immediately commenced an internal investigation to validate his complaint.

Richard wanted so badly to talk to Caroline, but the doctors advised him to be patient. The next day, Caroline asked if anyone had come to see her. The nurse told her that many people had been to visit, but the doctors had not allowed anyone in since she had awakened. Caroline then asked what day it was, and the nurse explained that Caroline had been in an accident more than two months ago and had been in a coma ever since. Caroline did not remember anything. The nurse assured her that she was recovering nicely, and that her memory would come back with time.

After being notified of Caroline's improvement, the doctors agreed that Richard should be allowed to visit with her. Richard went in the middle of the night to avoid reporters. Because of his connection with his girlfriend nurse, who still worked at the hospital, Michael Wilson knew of Richard's visit and was there when he arrived. Wilson approached Richard, but seeing the look on Richard's face, Wilson backed off. Doctors warned him not to push Caroline to answer any questions, that her memory was not back yet, and they did not want her to regress.

Richard walked into the room, where Caroline sat on her bed propped up with pillows. The nurse had helped her comb her hair and wash her face, and it was obvious to Richard that she was feeling much better. She smiled as soon as she saw Richard, her eyes filling with tears.

"Hey now," Richard said, "You are going to get me into trouble! The doctors told me I was not supposed to upset you. What are they going to say if they walk in and you're crying?"

He walked over and gave her a big hug. "How are you feeling? You look so much better than the last time I saw you."

Caroline smiled, and hugged him back. "I am getting better. These are happy tears. I am not upset, I am just really glad to see you. I'm sorry I can't help out with your campaign in this condition, but you'll see, I'll be back to work in no time!" She spoke slowly, haltingly, as if speaking was a long-remembered memory.

"Don't you worry about it. You just work on getting well. Once you are, then you can get back to work at the campaign office," said Richard.

"Last thing I remember was going to the club, after your announcement party. What happened? Was anyone else hurt in the car accident? Is Doug okay, and Jeremy? Did Beth or Kevin get hurt?"

"Everyone else is fine. You were the only one injured. You're not supposed to try too hard to remember anything because that will only slow down your progress, so don't worry about it right now. They have all been in to visit you. Once you are well, they will fill you in on the details of the accident, okay?"

Caroline wiped her sleeve across her eyes. "Okay, well don't you waste your time worrying about me. You get out there and work on your campaign, and I will join you when the doctors let me out of here, okay?"

"You've got it!" replied Richard, and reached over and gave her a kiss on the cheek. He told her he would stop in the next day to see her again.

Reporters mobbed Richard as he left the hospital. Michael Wilson may have backed off Richard earlier, but in the meantime he had been busy making calls. This was news again, after all. The mystery girl was awake!

One reporter yelled out, "We know you were allowed in to talk to her, what did she say?"

Richard looked over at him and answered, his voice heavy with sarcasm, "Thank you so much for your kind concern."

Then more seriously, "Her health is greatly improving. The doctors have seen improvement in her condition every day. I thought she looked much healthier today than the last time I saw her. Thank you for asking," and walked away without saying another word.

The next morning, Caroline requested a television set, and the doctors reluctantly agreed to give her one. They told the nurses to keep the remote, and under no circumstances to let Caroline watch any news broadcasts. She watched movies and soap operas, but during a commercial break of one of her soaps, she saw a news brief with Richard Johnson's picture on the screen. He was the subject of an editorial by one of the tougher political news anchors in the country, Shane Stansfield of CNBR.

She turned up the volume just in time to hear Stansfield say, "The mystery girl is recovering. Soon she should be able to answer the question, is she, or is she not Richard Johnson's daughter? Richard Johnson denies ever having any relations with her mother," Stansfield stated. He went on, "Richard Johnson popularity has plunged because of this scandal. It is a distinct possibility that he will not even show up in the voting during the upcoming Caucuses and Primaries."

Caroline was in tears. *'How could this have happened? What have I done? They said I have been in a coma for two months, what have I missed?'* Caroline thought to herself. She rang for a nurse, and when the nurse entered the room and saw Caroline's face, she knew something was terribly wrong.

"What has happened Caroline, are you in pain?" she asked. She rushed over to see what was wrong.

"I need a phone, right away!" Caroline cried, "I have to call Richard Johnson immediately!"

The nurse was not sure what to do. They had taken the phone from Caroline's room a week ago.

"I'll see if I can locate a phone for you," she started to say, when Caroline interrupted her.

"There should be one in my purse. I always carry my cell phone with me. Where is my purse?" asked Caroline.

The nurse walked over to the closet and saw her purse inside. She brought it over to Caroline. Caroline dug her phone out of her bag, but the battery was dead.

"Please, can you bring me a phone, right away?' she asked the nurse.

The nurse went out and asked another nurse if she knew where they had put the phone that belonged in Caroline's room.

"It is in the bottom drawer of the bedside table, but she is not to be making any calls."

The nurse went back into the room, and told Caroline that she was instructed not to give her a phone.

"I saw the news! I know what has been happening since my accident, and I have to call Richard!"

She started to climb out of bed, and the nurse gently pushed her back down again.

"I will find one of your doctors and explain what has happened. I'll ask him to come and see you immediately. You just lay back and rest, honey."

As soon as the nurse left the room, Caroline got out of bed anyway and walked to the door. She'd been walking with assistance during the past week; she felt a little weak and lightheaded, but was otherwise just fine. She opened the door to go out, and saw a policeman standing in her way.

"I am being guarded?" she asked. "What is this all about?"

The policeman explained that the press was very anxious to get an interview with her. He was there to keep them out. He also told Caroline that he did not think she should be out in the halls without a doctor or nurse, and asked her to go back into her room. Reluctantly, Caroline walked back to her bed and lay down. A few minutes later, a doctor and nurse entered the room.

"What's this I hear you have been watching the news?" asked the doctor.

"I know I was not supposed to, but I saw a newsbreak during my soap opera, and it was about me!" said Caroline. "You have to let me talk to Richard Johnson, it is very important!"

The doctor replied, "Caroline, you should not get yourself all worked up like this. I tried to call Richard, but I can't locate him. I did reach Sue Jacob, however, and asked her to come here right away to speak with you. Why don't you let the nurse wash your face and comb your hair while you wait for her, she should be here within a half-hour."

"Thank you Doctor, I appreciate your calling her. It is so important that I speak to her right away! I am not getting all worked up. I feel fine. I am just anxious to speak with Richard. Sue will know where to find him."

The doctor patted her hand and left the room. The nurse brought a warm washcloth from the bathroom and let Caroline clean her face. Then she brought over a brush and started to comb Caroline's hair. Having her hair brushed soothed her, and she felt better when Sue arrived a few minutes later.

"Been watching too much TV, I hear," said Sue as she walked over and gave Caroline a hug. "I am kind of glad you did, so you can explain this big mystery to me! We have DNA test results that show you are definitely related to Richard, and witnesses that say you claim that he is your dad. What is going on Caroline?"

Caroline and Sue spoke privately for almost 45 minutes. When Sue left the room she had a very confident expression on her face. She got on the phone and made several calls. Her first attempt was to reach Richard however she was unable to locate him. He was not at the campaign office or at the Governor's office; no one seemed to know where he was. She had tried his cell phone but without success. Sue called Caroline's friend Beth; then she called Donna, then the campaign office. She asked her assistant to call as many of Richard's Democratic supporters as possible and instruct them to remain close to a television over the next few hours.

She spoke with two of Caroline's doctors, and then called the four news stations and informed them that there was to be a press conference at the hospital in two hours. The doctors were reluctant to allow it at first, but Sue managed to convince them that she would not let Caroline get upset, and that this would actually relieve Caroline's stress and help her condition.

When she called Beth, she asked her to swing by Caroline's apartment and pick up some clothes, makeup and a hairdryer. She knew Beth had the key as she was watering Caroline's plants for her. She did not say much to Donna during their phone conversation other than to instruct her to get Richard, Michelle, and Doug together and have them in front of the TV in two hours time. For once it was very good news!

Beth arrived about 20 minutes later, and Caroline was in the shower of her room. Beth hung Caroline's clothes outside the bathroom door, pressed and ready for her to wear. When Caroline came into the room a few minutes later, she looked a little pale. She was trying to do too much at once, and it was wearing her out. She was determined though, that she would talk to the press as soon as possible.

She sat back on the bed, and let Michelle apply her makeup for her as she rested a bit. Beth then dried Caroline's hair. She looked better than she had since the accident. She was tired and a bit too thin, but the right makeup would hide the dark circles under her eyes.

Michelle had selected a blouse with buttons down the front, and a wrap around skirt to make it easier to get dressed. She also brought some sandals that Caroline could just slip her feet into. All this primping had made her exhausted, yet it was amazing how much better she felt having showered and dressed.

Donna had been able to reach Doug and Michelle on their cell phones, and they agreed to come home right away. She had a little more trouble locating Richard. He was not at the campaign office or at the Governor's office; no one seemed to know where he was. She had tried his cell phone but had not gotten an answer. She then happened to look out the window, and saw him sitting out on the dock. She walked across the lawn and out to where he was sitting. She sat down next to him, putting her arm around him.

"What are you doing out here, all by yourself?" she asked him, "I have been trying to find you for over an hour."

Richard laid his head on Donna's shoulder and replied despondently, "It's all over. All of our dreams of changing the world, of really making a difference in our country, are gone."

Donna gave his shoulders a squeeze. "Don't you give up now Richard Johnson, I didn't marry a quitter! We *will* get through this, and you *will* be the President. I know you will. Just come with me right now. Sue called over an hour ago and says she has very good news. The kids are on their way home, and we're supposed to turn on the TV in about 45 minutes. It is not over until it is over, and you are no quitter! Cheer up and get that positive attitude back, honey, it is all going to be just fine. Let's go join the kids in front of the TV. Come on!"

Richard stood up, and gave Donna a huge bear hug, and they headed up to the house, hand in hand.

Chapter 18

Revelations

The press was eagerly waiting in the hospital conference room, Michael Wilson at the forefront. Sue insisted on wheeling Caroline's wheelchair in herself with the two nurses walking beside her. The room was very quiet. Sue Jacob walked to the microphone speaker and announced, "Caroline Hoffman will be making a statement. She is not fully recovered from her accident yet. If you badger her with questions that upset her, the doctors will have Caroline removed from the room, and the press conference will be over. She will make her statement and will not be answering any questions today. You may ask her questions when she is released from the hospital and in better health. Do you all agree to these terms?"

The reporters all agreed, and, satisfied, Sue handed the microphone over to Caroline.

Caroline stared out at all the people, her eyes red from crying. She took a deep breath, composing herself, then lifted the microphone and began to speak.

"I am not really making a statement, I am telling a story. True stories which I had not planned to ever tell anyone in my life, but the events of the last two months have made it impossible not to do so." The room was completely still; no one made a sound as they waited in anticipation. Millions of people were glued to their TVs; Richard and his family were no exception. Donna was holding Richard's hand so tightly he thought it might break. Then Caroline began to tell her story.

"My mother died one year ago. She died after a battle with heart disease. After finding out about her heart damage, she knew she would not live long. The doctors could not do anything, and they let her know her days were numbered. She was too old and sick to have a heart transplant. My father, Greg Hoffman, died when I was six years old. I was an only child. Just before my mother died, she told me that she was afraid I would feel very alone in this world when she was gone. The only other relative I knew was my grandpa. He was in a nursing home and would not be alive much longer either. She kept telling me that there was someone very close to me living in Seattle, but she had made a promise never to reveal that person's identity until she died. She told me that after she died, I was to look in the bottom drawer of her dressing table and there I would find a box that contained information that would be important to me. She instructed me to never tell this information to anyone. She said she just wanted me to know that I have someone very close living in this world, so I would never feel entirely alone. Two days after she told me this, she died."

Everyone was quiet, waiting for her to continue her story. There was no noise in the conference room whatsoever. Caroline went on.

"A few days after my mother's funeral, I was cleaning my mother's house, preparing to sell it, when I remembered the box in her drawer. I ran up to her room and opened the bottom drawer. There was a blue metal box with a beautiful design on the top of it. It had been very carefully sealed with clear packing tape. I held it for the longest time wondering what was inside. This was a secret that my mother had kept for a long time, how long, I do not know. Now I would know, and I would have to keep her secret for the rest of my life. What a huge responsibility that was, but I simply had to know what was in that box. I carefully removed the tape and opened it up. On top lay a letter from my mother to me. It read, "My dear Caroline, I am sure you are reading this because I have passed on. Please do not reveal the contents to anyone, ever. Please destroy it as soon as you have finished reading it. If it gets into the wrong hands, it will hurt a lot of people."

At this point Caroline stopped for several minutes, then said, "There have been a lot of people hurt over the last two months as I lay in a coma by not knowing or revealing my mother's secret, so I must tell her secret to you now."

Caroline took a deep breath, and continued. "I read what was in that box over and over, and I remember every word of it. This is what she said, and how she said it." Caroline looked out at the reporters, and she had the full attention of every one of them. Michael Wilson had the sinking feeling that this was not going to add to his reputation, it would destroy it. He was part of this, as were all the other members of the media that had caused all of the problems with Richard's campaign, digging up half-truths and spreading gossip.

Caroline felt they did not deserve to know the truth to get a good news story out of this, but she thought of the Johnson family. She knew they were watching at this moment waiting for what she had to say. *'But,'* she told herself, *'the media certainly did deserve to know the truth, if only to preserve the right to free speech, so she would tell her story.'*

"This is what my mother wrote." Caroline closed her eyes to concentrate; she was greatly fatigued by this recollection. She began to recite what her mother had written.

"I met my husband Greg Hoffman when I was 20 years old. He was two years older than me, and he lived only one block away from my house. We saw each other quite frequently, and we fell in love. He was always good to me, and he made me happy. He had a nice smile that revealed what a good person he was. That was what made me fall in love with him."

"We were married when I was 22 and he was 24. We moved to an apartment as soon as we got married. Greg worked hard as an account clerk at a small plant. I worked as a nursing assistant. Greg liked to plan our future, and he said that as soon as we saved enough to buy a house, we would fill that house with children. I just laughed and told him maybe two children, but not a whole house full! He loved children, and wanted to have several. Three years after we got married, we were able to buy a house. Our next step was to start a family. After trying unsuccessfully for a few months, Greg started feeling ill. He went to the doctor and had some tests. The doctors told us that Greg had acute lymphocytic leukemia. Incurable at the time. We were crushed. He underwent chemotherapy and radiation and the cancer went into remission for some time, but the powerful chemicals left Greg infertile. The cancer treatment was working, but it took away his ability to father a child. Greg was very weak, and I continued to work full time to support us. Greg suggested we adopt a child, but I did not like that idea. One day a close friend of mine who worked as a technician in the lab at the hospital where I worked told me that if I wanted to make Greg happy, I should just have an affair with someone and have a baby. I told her there was no way I would betray my husband in that manner, but I also knew how much Greg wanted a child."

Caroline took a moment to dab at her eyes; then continued speaking her mothers' words, "She told me that they routinely received sperm in the lab for various reasons, and that it might be possible to implant a small amount in me, if we were careful, so I could try and have a baby without betraying Greg. At first I told her no, but I knew how much Greg wanted a child. This was the perfect solution! This way it was my natural child, and Greg would love it as his own. The next day I gave my husband's photo to my friend, and told her I would prefer the donor to look like my husband, so the baby would look like him, too, as much as possible. A few weeks later, she called me at my nurse's station, and told me to hurry downstairs to the lab. She had a patient that looked just like Greg. I rushed down to see and agreed with her. The man in the waiting room looked almost exactly like Greg! He was sitting there waiting for some tests on his prostate gland. Apparently he was having some pain and was at the doctor for some tests, one of which involved taking a sperm sample. Perfect! After my friend collected the sample from the man she did something called, I think, a washing test, which she said was standard protocol. After the test was finished, she took a small sample of the sperm, then carefully chose a room where we would not be discovered, and inseminated me. As I lay there, I was not sure if I could become pregnant; the chances were slim, because we couldn't use all of the sperm, but luckily I did! You were born nine months later. You were the most beautiful baby I had ever seen. Greg and I were so very happy. The person who came in for medical testing is your biological father, but Greg Hoffman was your daddy. He spent every minute of free time he had with you. He fed you and changed you, and sang you to sleep at night. He would not have been a better father to you if you had been his biological child. He took you everywhere with him, he loved to show off his daughter. Then when you were six years old, he started to get sick again, and this time he did not get better. You cried for weeks, asking for your daddy. You missed him so much. After your father died, I asked my friend from the lab for the name of the patient who was your biological father. At first she refused to tell me because of the legal ramifications, but I finally convinced her that I only needed it in case of a dire emergency. Otherwise I would take the information with me to my grave."

Caroline looked out over the gathered crowd with an intensity that belied her tired appearance as she delivered the stunner, "That man's name is Richard Johnson. He was a law student at Stanford University at the time. He is from Seattle, and the last time I looked into his whereabouts, he was running for Governor of Washington State. My advice to you is to never contact him, just know that you are not alone in this world. Richard Johnson is having a successful career, and he is a happily married man with two children. I took something from him without his knowledge or permission, and we should not interfere in his life."

The reporters all sat there in stunned silence. They were obviously not prepared to hear a truth being told that wasn't going to result in more damage to Richard Johnson. Richard, Donna, and the kids were silent as well. Everyone was in shock just trying to absorb this information and wondering if there were more.

Caroline began speaking again. "That was my mother's secret. She trusted me with it, and I have betrayed her trust, and ruined Richard Johnson's political career. Please accept my apology. I never should have come. I never wanted any of this to happen. I just wanted to get to know my biological father better, and help him to win his campaign. He is a wonderful person, and he deserves to be President. I have cheated the American people out of a great leader. I am so sorry. I will leave Seattle just as soon as I am well."

Caroline's body was racked by sobs now, and the nurses began to wheel her from the room. Normally the press would at least try to ask some questions, but they just sadly watched her being wheeled from the room, even Michael Wilson. They had gotten a great news story, but the real truth revealed a sad life story. Most of them left the press conference thinking, *Life is always stranger than fiction.* Sue took over the wheelchair from the nurse and pushed Caroline back to her room.

Sue helped Caroline out of her wheelchair and back into her bed, stating, "Caroline, no one will blame you for this. You wanted to get to know your father. No one can hold that against you. Anyone else would have done the same. The circumstances of your parentage are certainly not of your doing. If history is any indication, when the American people are told the truth, they are very forgiving. You need to calm down now, this is not good for your health."

Sue stepped out and asked a nurse to give Caroline something to calm her nerves. It must have just hit Caroline, the full ramifications of what had happened. She was inconsolable.

Chapter 19

The Truth is Out

Across town, Richard and his family were all joyfully embracing one another in a big hug. The truth was out, and none of it was Richard's fault. He now had another daughter, though. Doug and Michelle had an older half-sister. Donna had a stepdaughter. They all agreed they should go to the hospital immediately. Caroline was obviously overwrought with shame and blamed herself for everything. It was certainly not her fault; who wouldn't want to get to know their family? They all piled into the Jeep and headed for the hospital. They arrived and tried to push their way through the reporters.

"What is your reaction to this news, Governor?" This from Michael Wilson still determined to salvage a story that would take Richard Johnson down and make Tom Gibson happy.

"Will you try to prosecute the lab technician?"

"How are you feeling about Caroline Hoffman, Mr. Johnson?"

Richard could not seem to get through the mob anyway, so he decided to answer a few questions. He turned towards the mob of reporters, the damage from the past few months falling away. He again looked the regal leader that he was meant to be.

"I am, of course, surprised by the news as I had no idea any of this had happened. I am glad to have the mystery solved. I haven't given any thought to the lab technician. My immediate concern is for my new daughter, and how she is feeling right now. I am both pleased and a little sad. I am grateful that the truth is out, and happy to know I have another daughter. Caroline Hoffman is a wonderful young lady, and I am very proud to be her father. It's sad though that I missed out on 25 years of her life. I feel that was stolen from me and stolen from her as well, but the past is the past, and we can only go on from here. Please excuse me now, I really want to go to Caroline and see how she is holding up."

With that the reporters moved out of his way, and let him pass by. He went straight to Caroline's room. Donna and the kids waited outside to give them some privacy. Caroline was still sobbing as he walked in. He walked over to her and gathered her into his arms. "Don't you hate me for what I have done to your life, to your career?" sobbed Caroline.

"Of course not, Caroline! I wish you could have just come to me in the first place and told me the story, but your mother made you promise not to tell anyone. I know you did not mean for any of this to happen. You wanted to get to know me, and I am very thankful for that. The accident was certainly not your fault, nor any of the events that have happened since. It took a great deal of courage for you to hold that press conference today, and you did it to clear my name. I am grateful to you for that. I am proud to be your father. You are a wonderful person. I thought that even *before* I knew I was your dad, so I am not just biased because you really are my daughter!"

She smiled up at him through her tears, and he hugged her a little tighter. She stopped crying. Richard said, "You have a brother, sister, and stepmother outside this room that are dying to come in and see you. What do you say?"

"I say bring them in!" Caroline said, wiping away her tears as she laughed aloud.

Richard got up and went out into the hall to get them. Doug asked Richard if he could talk to Caroline alone for just a minute. Richard said that that would be fine, and Doug went in.

"Hey Sis!" teased Doug. "I wanted to talk to you alone for a minute before the others come in. I want to apologize for that night at the club. I was totally out of line, and I am sorry. It all makes sense, now that I know you are my sister."

"You don't have to apologize, Doug. I really overreacted. The accident was not your fault." Caroline took on a more serious tone, telling Doug, "If I wasn't your sister, I would want to go out with you though, you know. You are a really great guy. Beth really likes you."

"She does? Wow, I thought she just saw me as a friend." Doug mulled over this new bit of information.

"Maybe when I get out of here, we can go on a double date, me and Jeremy and you and Beth. What do you think?" asked Caroline.

"Yeah, that sounds like fun!" answered Doug.

"It will have to be soon. I need to head back to California. Richard doesn't need me around messing his campaign up anymore," said Caroline.

"Are you crazy? He is *not* going to let you go to California. He will be making the guest room into a bedroom for you and making you give up your apartment! He is already upset about missing your first 25 years. Believe me when I tell you he won't stand for your moving away. And by the way, you better not call him Richard anymore. You'll have to call him 'Dad' from now on. Should I let everyone in now? Am I forgiven, Caroline?" asked Doug.

"Of course, as if there was ever anything to forgive!" Caroline answered.

Doug walked out into the hallway and motioned to the rest of the family to come in.

Michelle raced over to Caroline's bedside and gave her a big hug.

"I can't believe I really have a sister! Now you and I can really gang up on Doug! Two against one!" laughed Michelle.

Donna walked over and took Caroline's hand. "How are you feeling, honey? You have had an awfully big day."

Tears welled up in both Donna and Caroline's eyes as Donna

continued, "Welcome to the family. I am really happy to have you for a stepdaughter. Thank you for holding that press conference today. I am sure it was not easy for you, but under the circumstances, I just know your mom is up in heaven, looking down on you thinking you did the right thing today."

"Thanks Donna, sorry Mom, that means a lot to me." said Caroline, "I am really glad to have you for a mother."

Caroline started to nod off a bit as the sedative they gave her was kicking in.

"Looks like this day is taking its' toll on Caroline. Richard, maybe we had better go home and let her get some sleep." said Donna.

"Yeah," Richard agreed, "we will be back here first thing in the morning though, okay?"

"I'll even try to sneak one of those raspberry muffins in that you like so much, okay?" offered Doug.

"I'll bring Beth and Kevin and Jeremy by to see you tomorrow afternoon, okay sis?" Michelle said.

"You are all so wonderful. I could not ask for a better family, really, especially after all I have put you through," said Caroline in a sleepy tone. "Thank you all so much."

"Goodnight Caroline!" they all said, and she was asleep before they were even out the door.

Chapter 20

Reversal

Almost immediately after Caroline's surprise revelation; Richard's poll numbers climbed back. This reversal was unprecedented in American politics but just reinforced the old adage that the *truth shall set you free.* Richard's former supporters called to apologize for doubting him and stated that they were behind Richard once again. Apparently, the American people still believed in Richard. After a whirlwind round of Primaries and Caucuses, Richard won enough delegates to push his nomination decision to the Democratic Convention. The cynic in Richard couldn't help thinking, *'Just as quickly as they leave me, they come back!'* Still, he was grateful that he had been exonerated in the eyes of his peers and the public.

Richard went on a massive tour of the country, re-energized by all the support. Everywhere he went he was met by massive crowds of supporters. All the naysayers had faded into the background for the time being. The pragmatist in Richard knew that just because this situation had seemingly turned out in his favor did *not* mean that he was in for an easy road to the Presidency. He just had to hope that his supporters in the Party and super delegates would nominate him at the Convention.

A week later Caroline was released from the hospital, Donna insisted she come to their house rather than her own apartment. After a couple of weeks, she felt well enough to go back to work. She rode in with Richard. When they entered the campaign office, everyone stopped what they were doing and gathered around to give her their best wishes. By mid-day she was feeling pretty worn out when in walked Doug, Beth, and Jeremy.

"Hi you guys! What are you doing here?" asked Caroline.

"We thought you might want to go to lunch with us!" answered Beth.

"I really should keep working; I have missed a lot of time since the accident." Caroline said.

Richard was walking into the room, and had overheard what she had said.

"You shouldn't overdo it on your first day back, I insist you take the rest of the day off and go have lunch with your friends. They have missed you, too, you know!" he said.

"Thanks Dad! I am going to take you up on that offer. I have missed them, and it is a gorgeous day. See you at home tonight!" Caroline said, and with that she was on her way out the door.

The press must have gotten word that she was at the campaign office because as they left the building, several reporters and cameramen came towards her. Doug stepped in front of her and started to tell them to leave her alone, but Caroline stopped him.

"No, I don't mind Doug; this will just take a minute."

"Caroline, how have you been since leaving the hospital?" the reporter asked. The media stopped reporting about Michael Wilson or Tom Gibson or Newman since Caroline's press conference.

"I am feeling better every day, and I have really been enjoying getting to know my family better. My dad is absolutely the greatest, and I believe that more and more as I get to know him better. I could not wait to get back to work on his campaign. I have always thought he would make a great President, and I am determined to do all I can to help him get elected to be the President of the United States. I will be the President's Daughter. Everyone has been so supportive since my story came out. My dad is more popular now than he was before, and that is saying a lot! Thank you for your concern, and for your support. We are going to get some lunch now. I haven't had a cheeseburger in months!"

With a big smile and a wink, Caroline walked away from the cameras. After they got into the car, Doug asked, "What was all that about, Caroline?"

She answered, "Doug, those reporters have a job to do, even Michael Wilson. If they don't get something for the evening news, then they are going to keep at it until they do. Dad's campaign needs all the good publicity it can get after all the bad publicity my accident caused. If I just stop and say a few words to the reporters every now and then, they will be happy. It's better to have them on our side, don't you think?"

Doug thought about this, and realized she was right.

"You have more of our dad in you than I realized smarty!" he said.

They went to Dick's for burgers, fries, and shakes and took their food to Green Lake for a picnic lunch. Beth and Doug took a walk around the lake, and Caroline sat on the grass with Jeremy.

"Now that we know Doug is your brother, I don't think he would mind if we went out together. Would you consider going on a date with me?" he asked.

"I would love to go out with you Jeremy! I have wanted to for a long time, but things were *so* weird. Beth has a thing for Doug, so maybe we could double date, and help the two of them get together." suggested Caroline.

"I don't think they need any help, Caroline; check it out," and he nodded towards Doug and Beth walking hand in hand.

"Oh good, I'm so happy for them. They make a great couple! Why don't we go to a movie tonight then, just the two of us?" offered Caroline.

Over the next few weeks Caroline continued courting the press, and Richard gained popularity every day. Richard made innumerable public appearances, showing off his "new" family, and the American public loved him for making himself so open and vulnerable. His family values first platform seemed to hit a chord with the nation.

Chapter 21

Democratic Convention

Finally, Convention Day arrived. The mood at Richard's house was exuberant. The past few months had passed quickly, with Richard's campaign making an unprecedented reversal of fortune. All of Richard's campaign staff had returned; he had brought back all the staff that had been laid off; as his funding had been restored and even increased to the point where he had brought on extra staff members.

Richard had also spent the past several months giving interviews at every opportunity; grateful for the opportunity to show off his family and speak about his policies and opinions as to what he hoped to accomplish if elected President. Vice-President Newman was paying the price for jumping on the "trash Richard Johnson bandwagon" too soon. He was trailing in the polls by a large margin, much as the Republican Party members who had called for then-President Clinton's impeachment. They had paid a similar price for jumping on a moral bandwagon without looking at their own actions first.

Richard's own Party members who had backed Tom Gibson were trying desperately to show him that they deserved Cabinet positions if he was elected. He truly was in the driver's seat and although he himself had a long track record of success in politics, he knew he had Caroline to thank as well.

Richard took Caroline to as many of his interviews as her

health would allow; she still had a tremendous amount of physical therapy to go through before she would be back to full strength. She reminded him of the Kennedy family; of how popular they had been and how their whole family had played a part in JFK's successful bid for the Presidency, both for the good and bad.

The American people seemed to love Caroline and all that she had been through in her efforts to meet her father, Richard Johnson. At every opportunity, Caroline shone like a star when presented to the public; she seemed truly happy to have found her family at last and they her.

As events had played out, Tom Gibson had watched in dismay as Richard had been exonerated. He was glad on the one hand that he had stuck to his promise to Richard not to publicly come out and bash him, but he had been deeply hurt that the rest of his Party members had been so quick to withdraw their support of him and return to Richard's camp.

For the first time in his political career, he felt weary of all the games and the back-alley deals that had gotten him to this point. He truly felt like "sloppy seconds" to Richard, especially now that Richard had proven to be truthful all along. Gibson wondered if Richard would live up to his promise; it had been a promise made in desperation, after all. Only time would tell.

Vice-President Newman's camp wasn't any happier than Tom Gibson's. Newman had seen Richard's predicament as the perfect opportunity. He did not include in his belief system that Richard might actually be an honest politician. That lack of faith in the very system that made Newman's career successful was now proving to be his undoing. He had attacked too soon and the realization of the enormity of his mistake was hard for him to fathom.

He sat in his dark office now, his thoughts gloomy. *'My one real chance to lead and I blew it!'* He thought back to earlier in the day, when his campaign speech had all but conceded the election to Richard. Tom Gibson and Newman realized that he had vastly under-estimated the American public's ability and desire to forgive a politician when the truth was told.

The Democratic convention began. Powerful Democratic senators commenced with speeches praising Richard's family for their valor and courage. The Johnsons had remained united to the end providing Richard with a chance to prove that he been totally truthful. State by state poles had been counted resulting with Richard being nominated as the candidate for the Democratic Party for the Presidency.

Michael Wilson had lost his appetite for politics altogether. His profession had almost cost his girlfriend her job at the hospital; she had been lucky just to be re-assigned to a different ward. In the end, Michael himself had been vilified by his own editors for reporting half-truths about Richard Johnson. Michael had tried to tell himself, and them, that he was just doing his job, but the reality was that he honestly did not want to be a political reporter anymore. He had turned in his resignation letter to his editor a few days earlier. Now he sat in his apartment, looking at all the boxes of his stuff packed and ready to go. The movers would be here in the morning to haul his things to Fresno, California, where Michael had gotten a job with the local paper, The Fresno Bee. They had a reputation as being a liberal rag of a paper and they had promised him the beat reporter position that dealt with local news only.

Michael reflected that this would be a nice change of pace from national reporting. Fresno had seemed like a nice mid-sized town that still thought of itself as a small town. They had their intrigues, but all in all, this seemed to be a good place to start over.

Chapter 22

The President's Daughter

Sue Jacob walked into Richard's office, exclaiming, "Governor, great news! The latest polls have you at 80% approval by the public for President. Newman has all but conceded the election. Caroline's speeches are inspiring; the people seem to really like her. She's talking to every reporter she encounters." Sue paused, reflecting. "You know, she's going to win this for us."

Richard sat back in his chair, his thoughts turned on all that had happened over the past months. He had gone from contender to loser and back to contender again; all over a mysterious girl that had appeared in his life with no warning. *'American politics is never boring,'* he thought. *'Who would have thought that I didn't have to actually win to be elected? Oh well, if dubya jr. can win that way, so can anyone!'*

At that moment Caroline walked into his office, practically running over to where Richard sat.

"Have you seen the polls, Dad? You're a lock!"

Richard loved her enthusiasm. She sat in his lap and he looked her in the eyes. This one person, this mysterious girl that had just popped into his life had changed him forever. He wanted to be President; he had worked most of his adult life headed towards that very thing. But this discovery of a daughter and the way it had all played out was more rewarding than anything else he could think of. His family had grown his decision to make his family a huge part of his campaign; they both had paid off handsomely.

Richard thought back to a recent conversation with the rest of his family. He had asked Doug and Michelle to express how they felt about having a new sister.

Michelle had exclaimed, "Dad, you know we like her and we love her!"

"Yeah, Dad!" Doug had chimed in.

Richard had looked at the two of them; they were the light of his life. But taking in a new family member couldn't possibly be that easy for them.

"You both are sure?" Richard had looked at both of them in turn. "She hasn't been a part of this family before the campaign. I need to know that you both are willing to make her a *real* part of this family."

Doug and Michelle had glanced at each other, then Doug had replied, "Dad, Michelle and I know that it will take time to accept her fully. But she *is* a part of you, just like we are, and we're both willing to work at it. Don't worry, okay?"

Michelle had nodded her agreement. "Dad, we didn't get this far by not being able to handle new things, no matter how weird or difficult they might be. Trust us."

Richards' thoughts returned to the present. He looked deeply into his newly found daughters' eyes.

"Are you ready for this?"

Caroline replied, in a tone that meant business, "Of course I am, Dad. After all, I *am* the President's daughter!"

Chapter 23

Presidential Victory

It was finally the Presidential Election Day. Richard and his family were watching the TV coverage until well over midnight joined by Sue Jacob, the Campaign Manager. By the next morning the winner would be announced. The 5:00 p.m. news coverage had indicated 80% of the votes were for Richard Johnson with votes having been counted late into evening in the West. The next day it was abundantly clear Richard won the Presidential election. He had in fact won every state in the country.

Vice-President Newman was paying the price for jumping on the "trash Richard Johnson" bandwagon too soon and was trailing in the polls by a large margin, much as the Republican Party members who had called for then-President Clinton's impeachment. They had paid a similar price for jumping on a moral bandwagon without looking at their own actions first.

Next morning at the Democratic Party campaign headquarters everyone was anxiously waiting for Richard to appear. The crowd of supporters was enormous. Newman had called Richard and conceded defeat earlier in the evening. It was time for the newly elected President to address the people. Caroline walked out to thunderous applause, looking radiant. Richard, Donna, Doug, and Michelle stood behind her as she stepped up to the podium.

"Please welcome my father, the NEW President of The United States!"

The crowd spontaneously erupted into thunderous clapping and enthusiastic shouting. Richard raised his hands, asking for the crowd to quiet down before he began.

"The people have spoken! Today is the first day of what I know will be a time of change, a time of greatness for this country! And all of you will participate and prosper!"

As Tom Gibson stood next to Richard Johnson, he couldn't help thinking, *'Vice-President isn't so bad. We will make a good team, despite what people think.'* Just like neither would admit publicly how they respect each other's viewpoints.

"I want to say thank you to my family, Donna, Michelle, Doug, and of course my newest daughter Caroline. With equal importance I wish to thank my Campaign Manager, Sue Jacob including all of our hard-working staff throughout the country. This moment would not have been possible without each and every one of you!"

Richard continued, "As promised from the beginning, the safety and prosperity of our country will remain my first priority. I extend an invitation to meet with those country leaders displaying an equal respect for human rights and to work closely with the UN on all foreign matters. I will increase the funding for defense to ensure our nation's technical superiority. The funding of every university, of private companies and for those working within the scientific community will now become mandatory. With this in mind, together we will work towards establishing superior defensive rockets, fighters and developing better laser technology. Private arm dealers including power hungry and fanatic politicians throughout the world will then be the losers."

"Secondly we will increase our intelligent gathering techniques with the highest of technology. As a nation we do not want to deploy our youth to other countries whereby many will lose their lives. We will fight from the air and from our bases in the United States. Our technical superiority will become the next decade's power base."

"Countries creating nuclear or chemical weapons or supporting minority suppression will be considered refusing to abide by the UN human rights policy. In working with UN imposing sanctions, our policy will be to cut their communication capabilities by destroying their satellites and precision targeting important military facilities. This will be the future defense policy of America."

"Americans will be respected worldwide by this nation imposing human rights with democratic values including strong leadership. We will continue to work closely with UN to maintain our Democratic values. As the world's most powerful nation I will uphold our belief in freedom, human rights and equality; I will not have it any other way."

"Minority suppression, genocide or holocausts will be stopped. No arm sales or training for countries like Sri Lanka."

The crowd continued clapping as Richard lifted his hands in grateful appreciation for their vocal support.

Richard and Tom Gibson walked off the stage to thunderous applause. As they reached the dressing room, Richard turned to him and said, "You kept your word Tom, now it is time for me to keep mine. I know you're wondering whether or not you will have any real power as Vice-President; I guarantee that you will. All of the things you have wanted to accomplish, now you can. Together we will make a great team!"

Tom was taken aback for a moment. He hadn't expected Richard to be this direct. As they had gone out on the campaign trail, he and Richard had danced around this issue.

"Thank you Richard. I have to admit, I wasn't sure what to expect. You are somewhat too good to be true to people sometimes. It's been hard following in your wake."

Caroline shouted out every where she went, "I am so proud to be the President's Daughter."

Every country in the world congratulated him. Richard's new American policy was well received and equally respected by dictators and communists including minority oppressors. Richard Johnson had fought hard with both grace and dignity; he was a sincere President that would make a difference not only within the United States but his impact would be additionally felt throughout the world.

www.ingramcontent.com/pod-product-compliance
Lightning Source LLC
Chambersburg PA
CBHW031941260626
47157CB00016B/1826